Cheesecake to Die For

Cheesecake to Die For

A novel by
RON ROSS

BEDELL BOOKS
Oceanside, NY

GOLDIE'S DIARY ENTRY

Dear Diary,

Would you believe it! I got my job back as the cheesecake counter-girl at Junior's. I am tickled pink. When I got back from Miami I swore I would never ask for anything else. You know what? It's true. You should never swear.

Hoboken's okay and I will always bear allegiance to the land of my birth but what can ever match the prestige and respect you command from running that cheesecake concession in the shadows of the Manhattan Bridge. And don't think it did not take a lot of courage on my part to call Mr. Harry Rosen and ask for my job back. After all, the way I left them high and dry. But I guess I'll just have to believe that I do have certain "special, captivating qualities and charm" that helped put the cake spatula back in my hands.

However, do not for a single second think that everything comes up roses when I am behind that counter. Remember, this is not a perfect world. Like today, for instance, my very first day back on the job and lucky I remember you have to keep that smile frozen on your face. There are these two guys sitting next to each other – strictly luck of the draw – who, I will call Happy and Grumpy as we were never formally introduced, although believe me, they were not dwarfs. They each order a slice of cheesecake which I bring back together, one in my left hand and one in my right hand, and daintily place in front of my clientele. As

1

Happy, with a big smile on his face, is ready to launch his attack with his fork already poised, Grumpy grumps, "How come he got a bigger piece than me?"

Truthfully, to the human eye, which I have two of, no difference can be seen but looking to avoid a major confrontation and being a strong believer in discretion as well as little white lies I answer with a very, very large smile that I do not cut the cheesecake and the cutting is done very scientifically.

I bear no ill will or bad feelings to such a person because I understand that to some men a little fraction larger is very important.

Anyhow, I am very happy to be back at Junior's and I will be even happier when people realize that I am not the one to ask what really took place at the Mermaid Social Athletic Club. Only the boys on the inside, one of the regulars at their card games, one of the daily shmoozers, like f'r instance Sonny, can answer that. Me, I am just a girl from Hoboken.

CHAPTER ONE

FIVEL FINNEGAN

Wherever anyone gets the idea that I am a "daily schmoozer", forgetaboutit! Maybe I'm not a nine-to-fiver – talking strictly about punchin' a clock, not laying odds, which also happens to be in my line of work, further dispelling the "daily schmoozer" tag – I'm just another hard-working stiff.

Also, I do not wish to disillusion anyone nor do I believe that everyone has to be a George Washington and never tell a lie, but I gotta set the record straight. If you have heard that I no longer enjoy a good poker game – do not believe it. It is an absolute untruth as well as being a most irreverant thing to say. Whoever would say such a thing may as well say I do not enjoy breathing, I do not enjoy sleeping and I do not enjoy eating, all of which nobody would ever believe about me just like nobody should believe such a story that I, Sonny LoCicero, who learned how to shuffle a deck of cards before knowing how to shake a rattle, do not enjoy playing poker.

In fact, having given it much thought, I think I even know how such a fairy tale starts making the rounds. Much of it has to do with one, Fivel Finnegan, whose personality, I must admit, irritates me about as much as a fingernail scratchin' on a blackboard. Do not get me wrong and think that my feelings for Fivel are of a negative nature. There are times when I actually smile thinking about him. Like when he is visiting his sisters and it does not matter which sister – the one in Arizona or the one in Miami – or when he is asleep or any condition resembling sleep. It is at such times that I have absolutely no bad feelings for Fivel.

It is only when I can see or hear Fivel that I start gettin' nauseous and queasy and my blood pressure zooms like it is gonna pop outta the top of my head. So, whenever Fivel decides to sit in on one of our poker games, I, who have no desire to suffer such symptoms, very politely say, "Excuse me, I gotta go to the toilet", which is a reflection of sorts on my upbringing, and even moreso on my instinct for survival.

Naturally, when I go I take all my table money with me, not out of distrust but it is just playin' it safe 'specially because I know I ain't comin' back. After a while, I'm sure the guys at the table are thinkin' I got a serious bladder problem or else I fell in the toilet bowl but bein' real sharp cookies they eventually figure out that I am gone for the evening. This does not happen once and it does not happen twice – it happens every time Fivel sits himself down at our table. It is only natural for someone with a good noodle in his noggin to make the deduction that a guy who keeps leavin' a poker game to pee and never comes back has probably lost his love for the game. Not a bad deduction, but I assure you, it does not win a cigar.

When Fivel Finnegan comes to a poker table you are not playin' poker any longer. Playin' poker is an art form that requires your full attention an' should be a relaxing experience because you gotta be able to conserve your energy so your mind can concentrate on two things – the cards and the players at the table. But Fivel winds everyone up like a tight spring an' you're always on guard, watchin' every word you say, makin' sure not to leave yourself open to one of Fivel's crazy challenges or dares. Soon you're afraid to look straight ahead so you're sneakin' glances from the corners of your eyes, you wind up sputterin' an' stammerin', all of a sudden you got large patches of perspiration around your armpits, and all-in-all, you are not havin' a good time. A smart person gets up, goes to take a pee, and never comes back – at least not while Fivel is there.

Not meaning to be irreverent, I got a gut feeling that once God got done creating man, his next job musta been goin' to work on the weasel an' Fivel hadda been caught in the change-over. By all the laws of Nature, Shamus Aloyisius Finnegan hadda been born into a family and at one time musta been a child, but I doubt it. I find it easier to picture him just happenin' – like from spontaneous combustion or whatever it is. He is a small, scrawny sack of bones with a chest like a chicken whose hunched shoulders seem to be hiding or protecting his body, whatever there is of it, for what reason I do not know because it is a body I am sure no one else would want anyhow. He has a sharp, pointy face that follows behind a long, needle nose which is always sniffing an' searching for something and is helped along by wide slits of eyes with two little balls constantly darting back 'n forth – it almost looks like they circle his head. Also, he musta turned his head when he was gettin' a mouth because it wound up on the left side of his face – an' he never hung aroun' to get lips. I do not think anyone carries his picture in their wallet or pocketbook.

So far, these are the good things about Fivel – what you'd call the plusses. It is his character an' personality that make it so difficult to love him – an' fills one with the desire to go take a pee when he is around. It is not so much that Shamus Aloysius Finnegan is a disagreeable person – he is more a disagreeing person. He disagrees with everything an' everyone. You cannot say the sky is blue without him challenging you. And it is not that he is a smart or studious person or even knows anything about what you may be talking about. He is like the guy who shakes in his boots at the sight of his own shadow but when he gets behind the wheel of a car this guy is ready to take on the world. Fivel has no car so he takes on the world by calling you on whatever you say an' he does it in such a way, it is like he is sayin' you do not know what you are talkin' about an' he backs you up against a wall so ya gotta defend yourself even if you don't want to because he puts in a challenge with money on the line an' is always givin' big odds that if you turn down, you look like a wimp. An' it don't matter how innocent a thing you may say – if it ain't an absolute, then Fivel has ya in his sights. F'r instance,

Fats Suozzo sits in on a poker game an' pushes away a bowl of peanuts that is in front of him with the announcement, "Keep these away from me. I am on a diet as I have met a doll that wishes to dance a little closer to me than she is now able to do." To which Fivel snaps, "Five'll getcha ten ya don't lose even five pounds in a month." Poor Fats is caught in Fivel's trap an' bein' a man of honor puts up his five spot an' is so nervous an' conscious of his bet that he gains five pounds. All he winds up losing is the doll an' his five spot. This is how Fivel flexes his muscle. It is always with that challenge, "Five'll getcha ten." An' that is why, wherever he goes, he is Fivel Finnegan. An' that is also why, ever since Fivel becomes a fixture at the Mermaid Social Athletic Club, our poker game, which was always filled with lots of laughs and story tellin' and was a place where all the Good-Time Charlies wanted to be, was now a very quiet, nervous kind of place filled with only "harumphs" an' "m-m's" 'n "ahs" but no real kind of talkin' – not while Fivel was around. Which, by the way, is the reason most of the guys put on a real glow soon as the temperature drops below freezin'. It ain't whiskey warmin' the blood – it is pure happiness due to the fact that we all know Fivel hates the cold. He hates it so much that as soon as he is able to see white breath comin' from his mouth, he is off 'n runnin' to his sister in Miami and he holes up there for the entire winter, and I do not move away from the poker table until after Macy's runs its Washington's Birthday sales and all the birds return to Coney Island.

It is not unwise to ponder the question why Fivel is not stepped on an' squashed so the whole year can be enjoyed like winter. Actually, the answer is a very simple one. You do not waste such energy on a flea, which is what Fivel was considered. Squashing, that is reserved for bigger, nasty propositions – real hurters, not little pests. Fivel annoyed. Yeah, he annoyed a lot, but he did not hurt. A guy who makes you sweat is not like a guy who makes you bleed. Also, Dwarf Langella, who is our trend-setter as well as our button-pusher, does not seem to care about Fivel one way or the other, which means the rest of us do likewise. It is true that the Dwarf does not sit in on our poker games and it is just as true that Fivel, like everyone else, watches his P's an' Q's whenever the Dwarf is around. That does not mean that what the Dwarf sees is a likeable, lovable Fivel because nothin' that Fivel does could ever make him such a person. Which brings us to the party of the second part, a real hurter, someone for whom squashing is a serious consideration, a guy who is really able to get the full, undivided attention of everyone, the Dwarf included – maybe even the Dwarf especially! If we are on a quiz show and the big make-or-break jackpot question is comin' up, about who can do the best job of drivin' the Dwarf up a tree, the whole audience would be hollerin', "Go for it! Go for it!" because there is not a person around who does not know that the only one who can make the Dwarf's face move and the blood run faster in his veins is Louie the Louse. I do not believe the Dwarf could ever imagine that some day his little empire, which revolves around the Mermaid Social Athletic Club, depends on what happens between Fivel Finnegan an' Louie the Louse - an', oh yeah, Goldie, the cheesecake girl from Junior's.

CHAPTER TWO

LOUIE THE LOUSE

Louis DeLouise, known to one and all as "Louis the Louse", is a piece of work that nobody would ever want to copyright or get a patent for. But if it was your wish to make him a fond memory you'd have to get on a line like you were goin' to the Christmas show at Radio City Music Hall. The point is, everybody wants to get on that line – but the truth is, tickets do not sell too good because when it comes to facin' up to this Dale Carnegie dropout, everyone remembers they had a previous engagement.

Most people feel that nothin' or no one can really rattle the Dwarf and I guess that's how you should feel about someone who's big enough to dance with the Statue of Liberty and strong enough to flip her over his shoulders if they were doin' a Lindy Hop but all things bein' considered, we are still dealin' with a human being; a large, economy-size one to be sure, but a mere mortal nevertheless. Whether the same category can be used for Louie the Louse, I am uncertain but one thing I do know – an' that is, he is in a class by himself.

Louie has one of these big, round beefy faces that keeps him from ever gettin' lost because it is so red, that together with his red plaid vest, the one he bamboozles from Knuckles McTavish, he shines in the dark. Much of this face is taken up by a large, full mouth turned way up at the corners into what looks like a perpetual smile only you get this very strong feeling that it is not a smile at all, but somethin' very different. You do not expect a Greek or Roman nose on such a face and you do not get one. There is this boneless blob that gives very good access for Louie's fat fingers to go on long, extensive searches, which they do very often, never returning with gold; and his large, grey eyes, crinkling at the corners add to this look of that which is really not a smile. It was not too very long ago that Louie the Louse was just another one of the boys at the Mermaid Social Athletic Club, earning his keep by workin' for the Dwarf, which was the natural order of things. He had his area to run slips for the numbers, make collections from the establishments that had our pinball machines, slots an' jukeboxes an' most of his time was free to play poker an' pinochile an' go to the track. In other words, he had a really good life, somethin' to be truly thankful for. Only this was one very greedy person. Licking the pot was not good enough. Louie wanted everything in the pot. Which brings us to another pot-licker of great renown, his fame as such only exceeded by his reputation as a fashion plate of dubious distinction – the once-proud possessor of the only red plaid vest of its kind around, Knuckles McTavish.

Knuckles wanted everything the Dwarf had but bein' a realist, settled for runnin' a crap game in Bath Beach. It is said that shortly after arrivin' here from the old country his left-behind lady love sends him this vest as a token of revenge for the jilting she has received. Its red was redder and its plaid ... well, plaidier and it was so loud that when you looked at it, you actually heard it - it screamed at you. But it does not go totally unadmired. Louie the Louse looks like his jaw is unhinged the way his mouth just hangs open whenever he sees Knuckles' attire. If a person can look at clothes with lust, then that is what Louie does. There is this day, quite a while ago, that Louie, who is a frequent player at Knuckles' game, has this run of really cold dice. Because he is one of the Dwarf's boys he has no problem gettin' a marker from Knuckles. Only problem is, Time marches on, an' Louie does not pay off on his marker. It becomes necessary for Knuckles to talk to Louie in a way that cannot exactly be described as grandfatherly. Such a talk brings about a meeting between Knuckles and Louie the Louse which Knuckles assumes will be of a very constructive nature and result in Louie the Louse wiping his slate clean. After this meeting Knuckles takes leave of us to visit his family and friends in Scotland we are told by Louie and as a parting gesture of patched up friendship, gives to Louie the red plaid vest. McTavish must have a very strong fondness for the old country because we never see him again. Louie the Louse has just as strong a fondness for the vest as he never removes it from his person. When McTavish leaves the scene many eyebrows are raised an' the eyes below those brows all seem to look in the direction of the Dwarf. Maybe it is only natural to assume that it is the top guy who gains the most when the next-to-the-top guy is no longer around. Small fry fish like Louie the Louse is at this time do not raise eyebrows.

The Dwarf has this face that looks like it was chopped and chiseled outta an oak tree, of which he is about the same size – Whack! Whack! ... a coupla eyes cut real deep inta the head ... Chop! Chop! ... a nose with a few bumps here 'n there – it's good enough, leave it alone – an' Slash! Gash! ... a mouth! The rest of the tree gets a coat an' a hat and there ya got it – the Dwarf ! Gettin' back to the face – it does not move; and if you're gonna do somethin' to make it move, especially like causin' the nose to twitch or the corners of the mouth to turn down, you gotta be either a very stupid person or a very brave person. I do not know if Louie is brave or stupid or maybe a combination of both but I do know that he does things that make the Dwarf's face move. I cannot think of anyone else who can do such things or even anyone else who wants to do such things. Nobody is jealous of what Louie can do.

It is like one day he is a trusted employee, takin' orders from the Dwarf like everyone else and the next day he is in business for himself, only he is doin' business from his boss' store which is very, very unhealthy considerin' who his boss happens to be. About two or three months ago he does not come into the Club for almost a week. Not that anyone is goin' to go on a cryin' jag because they miss him, but the Dwarf has to get his policy slips so he sends out a couple of the boys to cover Louie's turf only to find out that Louie's turf has already been covered – by Louie himself. There is not much happiness in the Mermaid S.A.C. when the Dwarf finds out his domain has been invaded by family. And there is much less happiness when a coupla Louie's regulars come in to inquire about their payoffs. It seems Louie does not take over the entire business – only the pick-up part.

The Dwarf has his own code and his own way of doin' things. No way is he gonna let anyone know there is trouble in his family so he pays off without battin' an eyelash, which under any circumstances would be a physical impossibility as the Dwarf does not have eyelashes, nor does he need them because any self-respectin' bug or even dust speck would think twice before even dreamin' about intrudin' upon the Dwarf's eyeballs.

We soon learn that Louie is a much more ambitious guy than any of us would ever have believed. It is not enough to dip into the numbers pot, so Louie goes aroun' to all the locations that have the Dwarf's gambling machines an' makes his collections while havin' everyone believe he is still frontin' for the Dwarf – business as usual. The fact that the Dwarf is too proud to let it get out that anyone would dare cross him in such a way does not make this such a difficult thing for Louie the Louse to pull off.

Now, I would never compare takin' anything from the Dwarf to takin' candy from a baby but I really think that's how Louie is lookin' at the situation. It is no one or two day toot that he goes on but he makes himself a partner in the Dwarf's business. Every week or so another one of the boys reports in that his territory was visited by Louie the Louse. We cannot believe that the Dwarf just sits back and waits like nothing is wrong. But as the Dwarf does not need anymore raised eyebrows or eyes starin' in his direction right now he doesn't have too much choice but to be one very patient person. He reminds us of Mount Vesuvius and we are just waiting for the eruption.

Guys like us learn from a very early age not to look too far past the end of our own nose because what's out there we are usually better off stayin' away from anyhow. Also, what we do not see cannot surprise

us very much but as much as we try to look the other way it is becomin' harder and harder to believe that the Dwarf will just sit back and
let Louie the Louse move in on him the way he has been doin'. The
eye-opener here is that someone is actually steppin' on the Dwarf's toes
and laughin' up his sleeve about it, not that the guy doin' the steppin' is
Louie because, after all, he is the only one we would ever believe could
even dream of doin' such a thing anyhow. I mean this is the same Louie
who as a kid was drummed out of the Boy Scouts because his troop
leader found out that his idea of doin' a good deed daily was to walk an
old lady across Surf Avenue, through all the heavy traffic, then leave her
stranded in the middle of the street while he would run away squealin'
like he just got locked in the candy store overnight. But he was very fair
in tallyin' up his good deeds because he only gave himself credit for half
a good deed in such a case. So to get a full good deed he had to make
sure to leave two old ladies stranded in traffic an' ya should know –
Louie the Louse never came back with fractions on his good deed count.

But do not think of Louie as not being a sensitive, compassionate
human being with no feeling. Even as a little kid he devoted himself to
makin' sure that God's little creatures received decent burials. It was
not an uncommon sight for us to see him carryin' everything from field
mice to kittens 'n seagulls and buryin' them in the soft ground by Coney
Island Creek. His feelings were deeply wounded when the ASPCA
pointed out this was most inappropriate when done with animals that
have not yet expired.

As Louie grows up he does not change much but things in our neighborhood do change and much of the reason for this is because of Louie.
F'r instance, you useta be able to just pick up a newspaper from the
newsstand in front of the candy store and leave your change right on
top. No more. Now ya gotta go inside to get your paper and plunk
down your money at the cash register. That's because Louie assumes all
the money sittin' outside on the newsstand is there for him and he would
walk aroun' the neighborhood scoopin' up all the change from all the
candy stores. Lucky for Louie he has a good pair of suspenders – other-
wise his pants would be draggin' around his ankles. Also, you useta be

able to send a kid down to the bakery, or go yourself, for a few rolls and say "Put it on my bill" or "Charge it". It's cash on the line now; almost every store has a sign behind the counter sayin' "No Credit!" Blame Louie for that one, too. He'd go from store to store, take whatever he wanted an' walk out sayin', "Just put it on my tab." Naturally, Louie's tab only grew – it never shrank at all. And when Louie walks down the street he never has to worry about bumpin' into anyone. He does not attract crowds. All the mothers call their kids in to do their homework, have dinner or any excuse they can come up with to get them off the street when they catch sight of Louie. I know that stray dogs and alley cats probably do not do homework so for them it is probably just good instinct to make themselves scarce when Louie comes around.

CHAPTER THREE

HERMAN AND MINNIE

So, although the Dwarf sits back and waits, looking like he is doin' nothing, we are sure he is thinkin' overtime about Louie the Louse, which is why one like Fivel Finnegan is no more important than a flea speck to him. In fact, when Louie first moves in on the Dwarf's action, it is Fivel who points out that no one, not even the Dwarf, should be surprised because it is very normal for Louie the Louse to be abnormal. It is due to such behavior that Herman the Hackie is no longer with us and the Widder Brown drives his cab by braille and I utter Herman's name only with the deepest respect and admiration because he worked so hard an' faithfully at his job that he made the rest of us hide our heads in shame every time we sat down at a card game or shot a game of pool .We all blame Louie for what happened to Herman Brown but the truth is, if the Dwarf is a little less generous in takin' care of his own Herman would probably still be drivin' his hack and Minnie Brown would still be doin' what she does best – sellin' newspapers and flowers.

Herman was a very likeable sort of a guy because he did not have enough time to do anything unlikeable. He worked around the clock, drivin' a Yellow Cab day and night, seven days a week and he musta owned a very oversized watch because his day had a lot more than twenty-four hours. Why he worked so hard, no one could ever figure out. Here was a guy that did not even have to pay rent if he didn't want to because he an' Minnie were never home anyhow. While he was driving customers around the city Minnie was sellin' newspapers all day long from her little stand on the corner across from the Mermaid Social Athletic Club. And at night she'd make the rounds of all the restaurants and bars sellin' flowers. We could never figure out which was older – her flowers or her newspapers; but like Fivel Finnegan said, "Her price wuz right!" The first time Fivel buys a paper from Minnie, which is quite some time ago, and remember – he is still a steady customer – she is barkin' out, " Get yer mornin' paper! Daily News an' Daily Mirror – only two cents! "

Fivel knows a bargain when he sees one because everywhere else these papers are sellin' for three cents an' never before does he see a price war between newsies. Anyhow there are many newsworthy items for Fivel to read up on, such as the morning line at Belmont so he plunks down his two cents and walks off with his paper. It is not even three minutes later when he comes runnin' outta the Club, shoutin' , " Hey, lady, today is Friday! "

Minnie smiles this big, gap-toothed smile at him. "You learn that from readin' my paper? Ain't education a wunnerful thing?"

"How could I learn such a thing from your paper, when it is Thursday's paper?"

"But it is the whole, complete paper and one-third off on the price," Minnie explains.

"It ain't the right news," an exasperated Fivel shouts.

"Why? You mean all of that stuff didn't happen?" Minnie asks in wide-eyed innocence.

"Sure it happened. But it happened two days ago. I wanna know what happened yesterday!"

So Minnie gives this shrug of her shoulders an' says with a sigh of resignation, "Look, I wanna keep you as a satisfied customer. You wanna know what happened yesterday? I'll tell ya what. I'm gonna give ya store credit. Gimme back this paper and you come back first thing tomorrow mornin' an' I'll have today's paper for you so you'll know what happened yesterday. Is that so bad for two cents?" Fivel thinks for a long minute, scratches his head, and finally getting a good grasp of what Minnie just said, starts sayin' "No" when Minnie cuts him off at the pass, wailing, "The whole world wants to take advantage of a poor, blind woman!" Minnie, who uses her cataracts like Joe DiMaggio uses a 36-ounce bat, has just knocked Fivel Finnegan over the left field fence where he finds he has a lot of company. Ya see, all of us read two day old newspapers because we are, and we don't want anyone to know, just a bunch of softies. Anyhow, when Minnie says it's the same news whether you read about it the next day or the day after – it don't change nothin' – she ain't exactly wrong.

One bright an' sunny day Herman the Hackie wakes up and realizes that things are not goin' exactly the way he and Minnie planned. In fact they have not seen too much of each other since their wedding day and as they have just recently celebrated their thirtieth year of wedded bliss by meeting for a fifteen-minute anniversary bash at Nathan's Famous, wolfin' down four franks with the works, it just reinforces Herman's thinking that maybe there's a better way. After sittin' an' figurin' feverishly in his cab between runs, scribblin' on a brown paper bag that still carried the sardine 'n onion smell of his noontime repast, Herman sees the light – capitalism beckons to him – he must become an entrepreneur! With the hours he works, Herman realizes he will become a rich man if he owned his own hack instead of dividing his fares with the company. His mind is already made up but as a devoted, sharing husband , Herman races over to Minnie's stand and out of breath from excitement, shouts to her, "I'm gonna be a boss, Minnie. Everything's gonna be good! I'm gonna be a boss!"

Minnie beams at Herman proudly. "Bein' a boss is a good thing. Who ya gonna boss, Herman?" For a split second Herman is stumped but then he smiles and thumps his chest, explaining, "Myself, Minnie, That's who I'm gonna boss. I am gonna boss myself!"

Minnie gives a nod of her head in quiet approval. "You're gonna boss yourself, Herman? That's a good thing, too. You follow orders very good, Herman. You should do very well bossin' yourself."

Now all Herman had to do was raise the money to buy a cab which Herman found out was not too hard to do as long as you had the money to lend to the bank so they could lend it back to you and charge you interest for it. "What is this collateral you want so you can lend me the money?" Herman asked the Loan Officer at the third bank he went to. All of them wanted the same thing from him – collateral! Maybe Herman should feel good because this guy talks to him like he is not Herman Brown the Hackie, but J.P. Morgan. "What we are asking of you is that you display your solvency." This makes Herman a little bit uncomfortable and he sneaks a quick look at his fly. "For example," Mr. Loan Officer continues, "if you would give us a car as collateral, we would probably consider that as acceptable."

Herman is now totally bewildered. "Before I leave, let me make sure I am understanding so I can explain it to my wife Minnie, who I know will never believe it, anyhow. You are telling me I gotta give you a car so you can lend me the money to buy a car?"

This is how Herman winds up coming to the Dwarf, sort of like the bank of last resort. It is not that Herman does not know the Dwarf or thinks of him as a bad person. In fact, the Dwarf has used Herman's services on numerous occasions, like goin' to the track or uptown to the Garden, so maybe it is time, thinks Herman, to use the Dwarf's services. Herman finds out that what he has heard is true – the Dwarf takes care of his own; Herman never thought of himself as one of the Dwarf's 'own' but he was very glad to find out he was. All he does is tell the Dwarf how much he needs to buy a nice second-hand cab, he signs a marker, and the money is in his pocket. No talk about collateral, a word which Herman learned to hate, and just a little friendly advice about payin' the monthly vigorish on time. In fact, Herman learned that even if he was late once in a while, it was no real problem as long as he explained it. Naturally, it cost more than the bank would charge, but as far as Herman was concerned, it was well worth it.

So, Herman goes in business for himself and suddenly there is a future for him and Minnie. He still works long, hard hours but this he does not mind because he knows what is waiting for him at the end of the rainbow. But as it turns out, for Herman the end of the rainbow is a much longer trip than he thinks it is.

Every month, after makin' his payment to the Dwarf, he is very happy to find out that he was right – there is a lot more left over for Minnie and him than when he was workin' for the cab company. Only Herman, without even havin' a pair of dice in his hands very soon rolls snake-eyes – or it is rolled for him by the Dwarf.

What happens is something that happens to the best of us and as no one will dispute the fact that the Dwarf is certainly the best of us, it is not so shocking – the Boss runs short of mazuma ... the green stuff ... dinero. When business is good, which is most of the time, the Dwarf does not smile because his face is not constructed for such things and, on the other hand, when things go bad - which does occur once in a great while – the face still does not move but the rest of the body does. Cash must be raised.

CHAPTER FOUR

THE MARKER OF HERMAN

The Dwarf does not like holidays because in his line of work, holidays can only cause problems. So on Lincoln's Birthday when the number "212" comes in and all the holiday-numbers-bettors who covered February twelfth run out and celebrate the Boss does not join in. He runs out to raise the cash to cover his payoff. The Dwarf's customers never are kept waiting.

The Dwarf does what he always does in such a situation; he gathers together whatever he has on hand, brings it to the Fair Deal Pawn Shop on Neptune Avenue and hocks it. Usually, in about two weeks he is flush again so he comes back and redeems everything. Sometimes, he gets lazy so it sits for a little over a month but not to worry – Honest Otto, the pawnbroker, knows to hold the Boss' stuff – the Dwarf will always be back. On this particular Lincoln's Birthday things should be no different, but they are. The Dwarf hocks his holdings, which are mostly markers, and the Dwarf's markers are considered negotiable notes anywhere that the Dwarf is known. Naturally Herman the Hackie's marker is included in this batch. Because this payoff was such a large one, it takes a little longer than usual for the Dwarf's barrel to get filled up again. But in about six weeks he is back at the Fair Deal Pawn Shop to redeem his stuff, only Honest Otto informs him between stutters and sniffles that there is nothin' left to redeem; that one of the Dwarf's boys, the one with the red plaid vest, came in the week before and bought it all up. The Dwarf picks up Honest Otto and holds him eyeball to eyeball, which means the hysterical – maybe soon-to-be historical – pawnbroker is quite a distance above the ground. He explains to the Boss how Louie the Louse leads him to believe that this time the stuff will not be redeemed because it was such a big hit and then he tells the Dwarf how Louie makes it seem like he had it all cleared with the Dwarf to buy up the markers himself. Still, Honest Otto did not want to sell out, he says, but pleads with the Dwarf that Louie the Louse can be a very scary kind of persuasive person. The Dwarf accidently drops Honest Otto who musta had a calcium deficiency because he winds up with two broken legs.

When the Dwarf returns to the Club we have this very strong premonition that Louie is goin' to be deloused but this does not happen. One reason it does not happen is that, for a few days, Louie is not around and we are told he is visiting his uncle in Staten Island. This I do not believe because I know Louie would not spring for the two nickels it would cost to take the ferry back 'n forth and if he does have an uncle in Staten Island I cannot believe he would let Louie visit him. Even Louie's mother and father do not allow visits by Louie. When Louie finally does show up at the Club he looks up at the Dwarf with that smile that is not a smile and tells him the whole thing was a big misunderstanding. He explains that he goes to see Honest Otto hoping to find his St. Christopher's medal which some lowlife swiped at the Baths only to have the fast-talkin' pawnbroker give him a sales pitch on buyin' this load of markers and such. Otto, he says, tells him in the strictest of confidence how the Boss, Donato Langella, (nobody calls him 'the Dwarf' to his face) is havin' some problems and would not be redeeming his markers and would like very much if someone he knew takes them over.

Louie is a very slippery eel sort of a person and goes on to admit to the Dwarf that he did not buy up the markers simply outta the goodness of his heart to help out his Boss – that just comes along as a fringe benefit. His uncle in Staten Island, to whom he claims he is very close

- although some of us are believing this uncle was just born - is in need of a good investment. So, accordin' to Louie, he informs his newly beloved uncle of this possibly once-in-a-lifetime opportunity and this uncle, who is naturally well-heeled, turns over the necessary bread to his trustworthy nephew and Louie, in turn, makes the purchase in his behalf. Unfortunately for the Dwarf, it seems this uncle is very happy with his purchase and will not consider selling it back to the Dwarf. Of course, Louie the Louse explains, he does not walk away unrewarded. For bringin' in such a plum of a deal he becomes his uncle's bookkeeper and collector – strictly a blue-collar job, he explains to the Dwarf. The Dwarf listens but like the rest of us, finds this story harder to swallow than a barrel of carpet tacks and as it is a story totally different than the one told by Honest Otto, the Dwarf decides to journey back to the Fair Deal Pawn Shop and see how Otto's legs are healing. Naturally, while there, he will again ask Otto to refresh his memory regarding the sale of his markers. However, when he gets there, there is no more Fair Deal Pawn Shop. The word is out that Honest Otto makes an extended visit to his family. This makes some of us think how much Honest Otto has in common with Knuckles McTavish and we begin to wonder if he will have as strong a fondness for his family as Knuckles did for his. Maybe it is only natural considerin' Honest Otto's two broken legs for certain eyes to once again look in the direction of the Dwarf just like they did when McTavish takes his powder. Why they look only at the Dwarf and in no other direction we find out in time but right now it is like every copper in Coney Island is a graduate of Scotland Yard. All they are mis-sin' are the hunting caps an' magnifying glasses. They spend so much time hangin' around the Mermaid S.A.C. we begin thinkin' they are charter members but the Dwarf is so clean that they can find out nothin' and after a while they let their memberships lapse which we do not mind because they are not dues-payin' members and they drink so much of our coffee we think maybe we have to buy Brazil an' Columbia just to replenish our supply.

The Dwarf has no choice but to let things sit then. It is not just that he is too proud for people to know there are problems in his family. He must be very careful about what happens in our social set because any-time the band starts playing, he is thought to be the conductor and every number is like a reprise of Knuckles McTavish and Otto the Pawnbroker. He has the option of either reducing the population even further, or buy-ing Louie's story and assume it was just a misunderstanding after all. This decision is helped along by the Dwarf's right-hand man and long-time adviser, Big Nose Sallie, who likes to have an ocean with no waves and does not wish to make a storm as long as you have a choice to keep things calm and peaceful. So Louie the Louse is given the benefit of the doubt that he believed the Dwarf was not going to redeem his markers and that he is employed by an uncle who somehow we sense we will never have the pleasure of meeting.

All of this takes place quite a few years ago and could be like wa-ter under the bridge but like Fivel points out – when you think back to that you are not too surprised about what Louie pulls now. Although it was not exactly party time for the Dwarf he does not get badly hurt and soon is back on his feet like nothing ever happens, but not everybody is so lucky. Like, f'r instance, Herman the Hackie, who never expects a smooth ride outta life but is lately gettin' one anyhow. Herman gets a visit from Louie the Louse a couple of months after the Dwarf's mark-ers are picked up and Louie explains to Herman that there is now a new set of rules. The Dwarf, it seems, gives six-month notes which he always renews as long as his customer is a good payer. But Louie tells Herman, that as his uncle's collector, he is advising him he gotta pay up his marker in full as his uncle made a bad investment and cannot afford to let things ride at so low an interest rate. Naturally, there is no way poor Herman can even dream about comin' up with such a number so outta the goodness of his heart and against his uncle's wishes Louie gra-ciously allows Herman to stay in business and keep his cab by simply tripling his interest payments.

That night when Herman goes home he starts figurin' out his new budget and after Minnie assures him that at the present time there are twenty-four hours in each day and seven days in every week he does not feel too good. That is because he has just finished calculating what he is making on an hourly basis right now and in order to pay the new interest rate he needs a fifty hour day and a ten day week. Minnie is not exactly a source of comfort when she shakes her head an' says, "I don't think they'll change it in New York, Herman. Maybe we can check with Jersey an' Connecticut."

Herman, who is now one very weary person, sighs, "It ain't easy bein' a boss, Minnie. It ain't easy." When Minnie thinks, it can be very dangerous and for one long moment she is in deep thought when she finally announces, "Herman, I can raise the price on my papers to three cents."

"Minnie," Herman asks, "who is gonna buy yesterday's paper when for the same price they can buy a new one at the candy store?"

"That's why you're gonna be a success, Herman. You have such a sharp mind."

Bein' that there is no way to stretch the days or the weeks, Herman figures he gotta work every minute of every hour of every day to even come close to makin' enough to cover Louie's payments. Beside his regular runs Herman starts hauling weekend fares up to the mountains, which in the summertime makes for a pretty steady flow of business but also has Herman's tongue hangin' out an' his eyeballs rolling to the back of his head. To Herman, sleep and rest are now just a memory from a very long time ago. But Herman is not tired and weary all by himself. It is like his cab, which is not exactly the latest model on the roads, is now wheezing and coughing like some tired old warhorse ready to pack it in. Before you get to Monticello, which is sorta the capitol of the mountains, ya gotta drive up this monster called the Wurtsboro Hill. It is something like the troll that lives under the bridge and ya gotta get past that troll to cross the bridge. Anyhow, the side of the road by the Wurtsboro Hill is like a graveyard for the skeletons of all the jalopies that do not make it to the top and Herman does not want his cab to be buried in such a place so he is very kind, considerate and helpful when-ever they start makin' the climb. As soon as the cab starts gruntin' and snorting, Herman says to his customers, "Ain't it a perfect time to get out and stretch our legs and take a whiff of the fresh country air?" And because they always answer,"No, we wanna get where we're goin'", he is always ready now with the comeback. "I cannot be so irresponsible. It is not healthy to change all at once from city air to country air. Ya gotta do it in stages or else, God forbid, you can overoxygenate which can lead to all kinds of things you don't want to be led to."

It is not that his argument is always convincing but he always wins because it becomes very obvious they are going noplace anyhow. So while they sit under a shade tree and suck in the fresh country air like Herman teaches them – "In goes the good air ... out goes the bad air ...", they witness a sight that makes them think that maybe it is too late and they are already overoxygenated because they are seeing what they know they really cannot be seeing; here is Herman the Hackie who not only can never be mistaken for a circus strong man but you wouldn't even mix him up with the grocery delivery boy when it comes to liftin' big packages, pushing his cab inch by inch up the Wurtsboro Hill, talking softly to it like it was a little baby with the whoopin' cough while a whole line of cars behind him are blastin' their horns and the drivers are sayin' things to him which can be interpreted to mean he is not their favorite person.

But the Wurtsboro Hill is also very good to Herman. Because of it he is always able to pick up an extra fare on the ride back from the mountains too. There is this place called the Red Apple Rest, which is sorta like a displaced persons camp. It is just off Route 17 before the Wurtsboro Hill and when Herman stops there on the way back to Coney Island for scrambled eggs 'n home fries there is always a group of people walking in circles with a two-day beard and an empty look in their eyes like they are refugees from some war and are walking aimlessly, but with no place to go, which is basically what the story is. They are the Legion of the Lost Cars. Their cars never made it up the Wurtsboro Hill and they never made it to the mountains to see their wives an' kiddies and it is now time to go home. So, every weekend Herman makes the drive back with a carload of these zombies, which is a big help in paying his nut to Louie the Louse.

When these stories about Herman the Hackie come back to us at the Mermaid S.A.C.our love for Louie the Louse does not grow and we feel that what Herman is doing is an impossible thing and cannot go on. We are right. It was impossible an' it does not go on. Labor Day Weekend is a scorcher, which makes for pushin' a car up the Wurtsboro Hill a very difficult task, indeed. In fact, with the ol' mercury scratchin' at close to a hundred even the act of pushin' a poolstick into a cue ball was a very heavy duty act, which is what I was doin' when Big Nose Sallie comes in to tell us that a reverse-the-charges call comes in from the Red Apple Rest to the corner candy store, which is from where Herman the Hackie conducted his business. The cash register girl at the Red Apple sniffles that one of their regular customers will no longer be dining there. When the candy store man inquires, she answers, "No, he is not switchin' to the Orseck Boys ", which is right across the road from the Red Apple. "Herman the Hackie will no longer be dining - period", she wails. She goes on to relate that Herman's cab expired at 10:03 A.M. No one is quite sure exactly when Herman expired because he was located some-where under his beloved cab at the bottom of the Wurtsboro Hill. She said that, strangely enough, he had a peaceful smile on his face, like you would expect from someone who would never again have to push a cab up the Wurtsboro Hill.

CHAPTER FIVE

THE WIDDER BROWN

Saturday's and Sunday's papers are not sold by Minnie that Sunday or Monday outta respect for Herman. As Minnie has never been married before and to her the prospects do not seem too bright that she will ever be married again she knows she gotta do some very compact mourning; not that she did not love or does not miss Herman but takin' the time to grieve and cry was a luxury and Minnie knew she could not afford luxuries. So, Sunday she gives a good cry and Monday she blows her nose and then puts it right back to the grindstone. First, she works out a real good package deal with the Laurenzos. She has Laurenzo's Towing Service haul Herman's cab back from the mountains and at the same time has Laurenzo's Funeral Parlor bring Herman back at no extra charge as they prop him up in the passenger seat of the tow truck which is driven by their son, Anthony. As it turns out, death is not always so certain. By replacing the radiator and carburetor and recharging the battery, the cab is brought back to life. When Minnie goes to the Funeral Parlor and inquires of Anthony, Sr. if he could do the same for Herman, the funeral director gives her a look that you think is gonna put her in the same place that her dear, departed husband is and says, "Do you not see the blasphemy you are uttering?"

29

"No," Minnie answers, explaining, "I got cataracts." Anyhow, as it turns out, neither Anthony,Sr. or Anthony, Jr. can do for Herman what was done for the cab so the wake goes on as scheduled and the Widder Brown shows us of what stuff she is made. First she tells us how touched she is that all of Surf Avenue and, in fact, all of Coney Island closes up outta respect for Herman – the penny arcades, the freak shows, the girlie shows, the games of chance, even the Cyclone – they are all shuttered and closed. We do not wish to disillusion the bereaved Minnie Brown by reminding her that Coney Island always closes down right after the Labor Day weekend. Even Fivel Finnegan acts like a human being when he shakes his head and says for Minnie to hear, " An' I'll bet they ain't gonna forget good ol' Herman for a long time. Five'll getcha ten they stay closed for better'n half a year." Naturally, nobody covers Fivel's bet.

It is at this point that Louie the Louse, glowing in his red plaid vest, comes bouncin' into Laurenzo's Funeral Parlor, lookin' like an overblown beach ball. "My poor woman! My poor woman!", he blurts, holdin' his arms out to the Widder Brown.

"If I am a poor woman it is mainly because of you," she says, squinting her failing eyes which are being further blinded by the shining brightness of Louie's vest.

"Is that any way for friends to talk to one another? I have just journeyed here to tell you that outta respect for the late, departed Herman and also outta the goodness of my heart I will remove, at my own cost an' expense the fiendish cab that did away with yer beloved husband an' also, I will not charge you any liquidated damages." Louie turns up his eyeballs to the heavens as he continues, "My uncle will hate me but I am just a softie at heart." It is then that Joan of Arc, Florence Nightingale an' Molly Pitcher wind up battlin' it out for second place.

The Widder Brown walks up to Louie the Louse and stands jaw to jaw, eyeball to eyeball with him and it looks like Louie quivers a little bit, but I think it is mostly because Minnie, like Herman, usually dines on those sardine an' onion sandwiches. "Soon as you touch my Herman's cab," she explains, " you will not be able to sell pencils, you will not be able to play the accordion, you will not be able to pick your teeth and if a fly should land on your nose you will have to call me and I will gladly come an' smash it for you. You will not do any of these things because you will not have hands to do them with." It is a speech that is so soul-stirring that Fats Suozzo is having a terrible dilemma choosin' between crying or cheering so he does a little of both. With tears tricklin' down his chubby cheeks he puts his fingers to his mouth and gives out with a whistle so loud and shrill that the crystal chandeliers that make Laurenzo's funeral parlor a truly class establishment, start vibrating and chiming and Louie's face is now almost as red as his vest as he realizes he is not coming off too good in this little tete a tete. If there is anything left to salvage Louie knows he better do it now and make as dignified an exit as he can so he explains to the Widder Brown that as long as she pays the interest, she can keep the cab. We all know there is no way Minnie can make the payments selling newspapers and flowers so we start passing the hat for her when she stands up and lets us know, "Minnie Brown pays her own way!" We point out to her that we can come up with a lotta cabbage as it is the Dwarf's hat that we were gonna pass around but Minnie's mind is set. She tells us she is gonna drive Herman's hack and sell her newspapers right from the cab.

Big Nose Sallie asks her, "How can ya drive around the city when you can barely see two feet in front of ya?"

"So I won't drive around the city," she explains. "I'll be a real neighborhood driver. I'll just drive these couple blocks around the train station."

"But ya still can't see!" Big Nose Sallie repeated.

"In my own neighborhood, what do I need to see? Do I look at the back of my hand to know it's there? Whoever is in my cab will let me know what's doing."

Sallie laughed, "Who's gonna get in a cab to drive just a block, tell me – who?"

"What a wonderful idea." We all turned around. The Dwarf did not speak too much, but when he did he got attention. "Just think of the shoe leather we save ... the energy we conserve for something really important ... the chance to relax a little more in a fast-paced world." We understood. We were all gonna join in on the Dwarf's guilt trip.

As it turns out, we do not mind this too much. After all, we are doin' a blessing by helpin' a neighbor in need and it sorta makes you feel pretty important takin' a cab to go just a block. Also, driving with the Widder Brown really gets your juices goin'. Such a ride in Steeplechase Park would be like a feature attraction especially when her passenger is someone like Joey the Clown who does not know his right hand from his left and it is his job to tell the Widder Brown which way she is supposed to be turning and what direction she should be going in. Eventually, Joey requests special dispensation from the Dwarf to give him permission to walk to the Club instead of riding in Minnie's cab as he is gettin' the shakes and becoming a nervous wreck. This the Dwarf turns down and instead has a couple of the boys giving Joey marching drills in the alley next to the Club until the Clown gets so good he could probably make the Marine Corps Color Guard. And then there is the case of Fats Suozzo who lives right next door to the Mermaid Social Athletic Club; Fats comes out every morning and walks a block an' a half in the opposite direction to Widder Brown's cab and then drives back to where he started. But the icing on the cake, the thing that really keeps us driving in Widder Brown's cab all this time is we know it's like givin' Louie the Louse a boot in the rump.

However, it is somewhere between surprise and disappointment to us that the Dwarf keeps himself in check and allows Louie to breathe the same air that we do. We tell ourselves it is a sign that the Boss has matured and mellowed with age and it is that he is a wiser, not a weaker person. But now that Louie has invaded his domain and still the Dwarf does not act, we begin spending more time wondering what is goin' on with our Boss than we do payin' attention to the cards in our hand. We do not have to wonder very long.

CHAPTER SIX

FATS, THE DWARF AND THE TATTERED WAIF

It seems Fats is carrying around this very heavy burden, that is, a very heavy burden other than the very heavy burden we are accustomed to seeing Fats carrying around. What happens to Fats is something that happens to him very often – he finds himself in a place he probably would be a lot better off not being at. And as Fats always found it a big problem figuring out what is okay to talk about and when to keep his mouth shut, he is having this tremendous struggle with himself because on the one hand he is dying to tell us what he saw and on the other hand he is afraid he will be dying if he does tell us what he saw. But when all this talk about 'what d'ya think is wrong with the Dwarf' is going around in the Club, Fats decides that if he is maybe gonna die anyhow, he may as well die talking which he enjoys much more than keeping a secret.

Every Monday morning Vito Fusillo, the only guy I know personally who pays income tax, drops off the leftover pastries from the Villa Vito which means that before Vito's car turns the corner, Fats, who lives right next to the Club, comes bouncing in whistling a happy tune. Without question, it is his very favorite time. But like I said, Fats is very often where he would be better off not being but by being there he gets a pretty good idea why it is like the Dwarf is handcuffed and shackled when it comes to Louie the Louse.

On this particular Monday morning Fats is the first one in the club as he always is on Vito's delivery day and he makes himself very comfortable as he squats on a cushion on the floor behind the counter where the espresso machine is. For company he has the tray of pastries that Vito dropped off.

But Fats has much trouble digesting his very first mouthful of cannoli because, although he is not surprised to see the Dwarf come in this early and sit down at a table at the other side of the room, as the Dwarf very often spends a full night at the Club doing paper work 'n such, he is unaccustomed to seein' a dame just walk in unannounced, without invitation, especially such a dame as now stands in front of the Boss.

Ordinarily, this would be unbelievable but as Fats sees it with his own eyes that is what we find out happens, plus a lot more.

It is very soon after the Dwarf pays off on Louie's absconded number plays and is considering the various ways of arranging for a Louieless world that he is visited by, the way Fats describes her, Cinderella before the Fairy Godmother waves her wand. This dame is wrapped in a pile of rags and has a hairdo that any sparrow would happily trade its nest for. She gets to say her piece to the Dwarf only because she starts off by telling him she is here making a collection for Louie the Louse's funeral, which is a cause the Dwarf would gladly donate to before givin' to the Red Cross, the Salvation Army or even the Italian-American Relief Fund. Although you cannot tell by looking at him, he is so overjoyed at this opportunity to part with money that he says, "Let me look at the body. I may even volunteer to pay the whole cost. I can think of no one more deserving of a nice funeral than Louie. How did his end come about? Was it possibly filled with much pain an' suffering?"

"Oh, it did not yet happen. If and when it does is in your hands. Louie is like a corpse-in-waiting and does not know that I am here. If he were to find out he would be most upset because he is not the kind of person who asks anything for himself. He is so unselfish," she sobs. "He says to me - 'Goodby, little waif. What I have done, I did for you and the forsaken children. I had to put food in your starving bellies and a roof over your heads. How can I ask Mr. Langella to understand that?' - He always spoke of you only in glowing terms."

The Dwarf, whose upset at now learning that Louie still lives so soon after thinking he was departed, cannot be hidden even by his face, says, "I do not have a very clear picture of what this collection is all about. If you are suggestin' that he be buried alive – okay, I can live with that, too. But all this talk about mistaken children ..."

"Forsaken," she corrects. "How can you speak so about a man so pure and noble of mind and heart? You would not believe how sorry he is that he had to take from you, who was always so generous to him. But in order to provide for us he had no other choice and even though he understands your anger and knows, because of who you are, that you will exact the ultimate punishment, his only concern is about who will now take care of the children. That is why I am collecting for the inevitable result of your vengeance - his funeral. This task has become my mission as he does not want any of the children's money spent on his departure. It is a promise he forced from me."

"I want you to know something," the Dwarf says. "I am once in a while able to do the whole crossword puzzle in the Sunday Times ... with a minimum of cheatin' and a little help from Noah Webster ... but I understood almost nothin' of what you just told me. I think what you are sayin' is you are askin' me to pay for a rub-out of which you are expectin' me to be the rubber-outer. But that cannot possibly be because that is an unthinkable request. Also, I am too much of a law-abiding citizen to be cast in such a role. Even so, to show ya my heart's in the right place, I am still willin' to pay the entire cost of Louie's funeral under the condition that he sets the stage by jumpin' from the top of the Empire State Building or a swan dive off the Brooklyn Bridge or some other very public unassisted exit from the world." It is obvious the Boss is seeking an end to Louie, but one that will cast no further stares in his direction.

"I cannot lie to you about how disappointed I am at your response," the tattered waif cries. "I was hoping to hear words of compassion spill forth from you."

Fats is sitting quietly behind the counter, unnoticed and still unable to touch his cannoli, as he is deep in thought trying to figure out this very messed-up doll. It is becoming somewhat obvious that Louie the Louse has trained her to be a parrot in what may be the super con job of the year. She is actually trying to milk the Dwarf to pay for a funeral, on one hand, and on the other hand she is trying to talk him outta the funeral – but not outta paying for it! It is no wonder Fats is unable to consume his cannoli.

"To leave these once-villified little urchins with no one to look after them ... How can your conscience deal with such a burden?" Fats says she talks with her hands flapping like a wild bird and her body swaying like she has the St. Vitus dance. The Dwarf just sits and looks at her in wonder.

"What is this with children? Louie the Louse is not a husband an' certainly not a father."

"That is the beauty of it," she is tilting and leaning at a most precarious degree as she sways and almost swoons while continuing her impassioned discourse. "Because of his own deprived childhood ..."

"The only thing he was deprived of," interrupts the Dwarf, "wuz a long stay in reform school."

This does not cause the now very intensely emoting waif to skip even a beat. "... he has dedicated himself to taking these poor, homeless young dregs of humanity and showing them love and tenderness by giving them a new lease on life in his home, just as he did with me some years before when he took me away from a cold, bitter, loveless world."

"He sure picked out a nice wardrobe for you," the Boss comments about her rags.

She is undaunted. "That is because we have fallen upon hard times and that is the reason why Louis did the things he did – it was for the children. He has devoted his life to lost and homeless children"

The Dwarf throws up his arms in exasperation. "I think you are misinterpreting very badly. Just because, if Louie the Louse, by chance, happens to be around any children he would be saying somethin' like 'G'wan, get lost, kid', this is not the same as devotin' his life to lost and homeless children. I am now certain we are discussin' two different people. In fact I happen to have a picture of Louie, two pictures – front and side view – it is not in very good shape because it was hangin' in the Post Office for quite a while, but you will recognize immediately it is not the Louie or Louis you speak of." He takes from a drawer behind the counter a folded picture which he smooths out and shows to her.

"Oh, of course it is Louis. Just look at the love and devotion in those eyes."

"Just look at the reward listed on top of his head!"

For a second she almost does a double-take, according to Fats, but then she goes on, like it is a dress rehearsal, "You have never seen Louis with the children because he is such a humble person," at which point the Dwarf almost gags and he is not even chewing on a cannoli. "He is not looking for gratitude; his only concern is their well-being. Feel for the little tykes, Mr. Langella. Where is your heart?"

If she was lookin' to push buttons, she has just pushed the wrong one. There are many things that the Boss likes – you can run down the alphabet and starting with 'A' you'll get 'Anchovies', 'B' you'll get 'Bolognese sauce', but when ya get to 'K' you will definitely not get 'Kids'. As far as the Dwarf is concerned, kids are nothin' but little people who make too much noise for their size. However, it seems this is a lady with some sort of insight as she immediately gets the drift that the Boss is not ready to take out his violin and play "Hearts and Flowers". She also realizes she is up at the plate with two strikes and maybe has one cut left so she closes her eyes and swings from the heels, "I guess I will just have to figure out how to explain to his poor, fading mother how God turns his back on her and does not grant her final wish to return to Calabrese for her eternal rest."

The tattered waif has now pressed the 'M' button – 'Mother' – and it is like the Dwarf takes an electric enema. His whole body jerks to attention and Fats swears even his hair stands on end. "What're ya talkin' about. Louie the Louse is not even on a communicatin' basis with no mother!"

Again, it seems like she is thrown into a state of shock but this is obviously one very resilient and resourceful creature. "He's not? Oh,

that is because she is quite hard-of-hearing. Very, very difficult to com-
municate with her ... but what do you think Louis lived for? What do
you think drove him to do the things he did? Actions speak much louder
than words!"

"I thought ya said he did what he did for the kids."

She gives a little stammer but in a second is back on track. "I did
... sure... of course he did it for the children. He did it for the children,
he did it for his mother, God bless her wasted body; his heart is so big,
there is room for all in need." Without realizing it, the Dwarf is wring-
ing his hands while listening to her. "What comes back to me," he
blurts, "is Louie does not even put foot in his mother's house, for one,
because he does not try an' for two, because if he would try, he would
find the door blocked by very heavy furniture."

"Rumors! Rumors!" She is shaking her finger in the Dwarf's face.
Actually, she is trying to shake her finger in the Dwarf's face but it is
really shaking at his belly button. "Only because she cannot bear her
beloved son, who worships the ground she walks on, seeing her in the
condition she is in."

Now you gotta try and understand the Dwarf which is not exactly
as easy as A,B,C or even X,Y and Z which is because you get no clue
by looking at him and I, for one, am a most happy fella that the Dwarf
does not sit in on our poker games as his face does not change from a
six high to a royal flush. Looking at him you do not get the feeling that a
person behind such a face is ever gonna pinch someone's cheek or give
a friendly pat on top of the head which, when you give a good look at
whom would be dispatching such tender signals does not fill one with
a deep sense of regret. So, if judging by such a face may cause you to
believe that the Dwarf is not a sensitive, feeling human being it may not
be a totally incorrect assumption but it will also not give you a complete
picture.

The Dwarf lives by a code. It is a very simple code as it consists
of only two words – Honor and Respect and it is a code that is instilled
in all of us. We each have our own priorities with the code but our one
mutual and top prority is to honor and respect the Dwarf and, in turn,

the Dwarf honors and respects us. He makes sure to take care of his own. But the Dwarf honors and respects no one more than the woman who brought him into this world. We have all taken note in the past that the greatest reverence the Dwarf has is for his mother. Like I said, it is a code that is instilled in all of us and that is why it is not a problem to understand how the Dwarf feels, but nobody shows greater respect or honors his mother more than the Dwarf. He makes Mother's Day the biggest holiday on the calendar. There are no numbers pick-ups or collections of any kind on that day; card playing is out – in fact, it is the one day of the year that the Club is closed to make sure we all spend the day with our mothers. If anyone's mother has passed on, then a trip must be made to the cemetery. If an ocean happens to separate you from the cemetery, the Dwarf is one very understanding person and permits you to spend the day in church paying homage.

Having extremely analytical minds we have deduced that the Dwarf, recognizing what is involved in carrying a load inside like he musta been as a baby, is forever indebted to Motherhood. Me, not bein' a trained, or even an untrained, psychiatrist, I cannot explain the whys and wherefores of such a reverance. I save a lot of time by chalking it up to being in our blood stream. Joey the Clown, who would've caused Plato many a sleepless night, I am sure, is of the philosophy that by the Dwarf's honoring and respecting his mother, he honors and respects himself. When Vito questions him about where he comes up with such an intellectual idea, he confesses to reading it in a comic book version of Ma Barker and her boys. Fats Suozzo, the only one of the guys who still lives alone with his mother, feels he understands the Dwarf's feelings best of all. "When you are born, you are very little." We are not in total agreement that this was the case when the Dwarf was born, but grasping very keenly onto what may turn out to be a pearl of wisdom, we choose not to interject such an opinion. "And even though you are crying you are probably very happy to be born as that is much more exciting than not being born." The pearl of wisdom hope is becoming more remote. "... which causes you to be very grateful and love the person that caused you to be born. Now this person keeps feeding you an' makes you grow an' the more you grow the more you love this person. That is why we love our mothers, an' as no one else grows as much as the Dwarf grows it is understandable why he loves his mother so much." We look at Fats and concede him second place in the Love Thy Mother department.

So, although we do not pinpoint the reason for such behavior we all agree there is nothing wrong with having such feelings as it is only natural to feel that way.

And that is obviously why the Dwarf responds the way he does to this tattered waif's tale of Louie the Louse's sacrificing all for his mother and it is with much concern that the Dwarf asks, "What is wrong with her?"

It seems that the questions now are of a much more difficult nature as again she does a little tripping over her tongue, "What is wrong with her? ... Okay, what is wrong with her ... It would require a team of medical specialists to answer that. That's how much is wrong with her. And everything Louis did was to make her final days as comfortable as possible and no cost was too great ... and whatever he did, no matter how unforgivable it seemed or how wrong it appeared – he did it for – for his mother. He knew it would not be understood by others but it had to be done – for his mother's sake. He asks no forgiveness for his deeds; they were done of necessity. He only asks that his mother be spared learning of his fate and that is why he wants to send her to Calabrese, so that she does not see what becomes of him. And that is why I am here, unknown to him, to raise the money for his funeral, which he accepts as inevitable due to your very justifiable anger. He is not even aware that if his money is used to pay for his own funeral there will not be enough left for his beloved mother's passage to Calabrese and her final rest. But I am aware! Has there ever been a greater tragedy befalling a mother and a son? I ask you, kind sir, is either deserving of such a fate?"

Fats says he was trying so hard, from the other side of the room, to snap the Dwarf out of what he was considering a spell, that he is bent over, going "Ooh! Ooh! Ooh!" until this waif, who he now believes to be a witch, and the Dwarf, somewhat startled at learning they are not alone, turn quickly to see who is "oohing" and why. She does not skip a beat as she stares at Fats and the untouched cannoli, then tiptoes over to him and offers him some Pepto-Bismol as she is sure he is suffering a terrible case of constipation. Fats takes his medicine like a man and wishes that there was some medicine that his boss could take. But he knows it is no use. As this tattered waif exits the establishment, she turns back one final time, beseeching the Dwarf, in his infinite wisdom, to off-set the cruelty of Fate. But the Dwarf just sits there, vibrating, his whole body wracking. It is a sight Fats is completely unprepared for, a sight and happening he never would have believed possible. He wants to go over and shake the Dwarf, but that is unthinkable as well as impossible. So he sits in his corner of the room vibrating and wracking, just like his Boss. He simply does not know what else to do.

CHAPTER SEVEN

JOEY THE CLOWN TO THE RESCUE – ALMOST!

And that is the reason why the Dwarf sits back and lets Louie the Louse get away with what he has done. Like I said, Fats is one very nervous individual about telling this story but he is so upset hearing the guys wondering what is it with the Dwarf, that he finally digs up the nerve to tell it to Big Nose Sallie in the back room. After thinking about it over night, Sallie agrees with Fats that there should not be a wrong impression out there regarding the Dwarf so the next day he decides to tell us what Fats sees an hears. Sallie does not, in way want to diminish the reputation of the man to whom he is so loyal and devoted, so he starts off by reminding us, "There's nothin' that I have to say to build up on what kind of guy the Boss is. That's because his actions – all the things he has done over the years say it all. But I know there's some talk going around asking why he allows a certain party to do certain things without inflicting on this certain party a very certain – and unceremonious - end."

"Well, now that ya brung it up," Joey the Clown cuts in, "we are also wonderin' why he lets Louie the Louse get away with what he pulls."

"You are a very observant person, Joey," Sallie responds with a half-smile.

"Not really, Salvatore," the Clown hangs his head. "The truth is, I ain't been to church in more'n three months an' that's only because Goldie drug me in to watch a wedding – sorta like a hint, you know." Seeing he is getting nowhere at a super-fast clip, Big Nose Sallie returns to explaining the Dwarf's situation. "Anyhow, the Dwarf, partly because of the person he is and partly because of certain outside interference, finds himself powerless to act."

"Whaddya mean by that?" Fivel asks. "Why can't he act? Someone holdin' a rod at his head or somethin'?" With which he gives a smile - on the left side of his face, of course, the only smile Fivel is capable of – and turns around to see if there is a roomful of smiles joining his.

Big Nose Sallie is havin' great difficulty explaining the Dwarf's predicament. "Maybe a rod at his head would not be so difficult for him to handle compared to what he is dealin' with. Like I said, an' I'm sure no one wishes to dispute it, they don't come tougher or more powerful than the Dwarf, but there is this problem – he finds himself unable to act because ... well, because there is a chink in his armor ... he is only human ..."

Joey the Clown is beside himself; it is not easy to look up to someone like we do to the Dwarf only to find out that he is just flesh and blood. "Whaddya mean?" the Clown bellows. "This is the Dwarf we are talkin' about. I cannot believe this! If he got such a problem, let's help him out. He would do the same for us!"

"When someone is so proud like the Dwarf, he does not wish you to know he even has a problem," Sallie explains, very impressed at the Clown's concern, "so how do we help someone when you can't even talk to him about it?"

"Well, then, you tell us," Joey shouts. "It's not like we do not know the answer, but we would like to hear it from you. How is such a thing possible?"

"To make it as simple as I can, Joey, let us just say that anyone can have a chink in his armor – even the most powerful of men – for instance, there is Samson, there is Achilles ..."

" I don't know what mob they're from an' I don't care about those jokers ... no insult intended if they are related to you, Salvatore," the

Clown apologizes, "but right now I only wanna know what we do to take care of the Dwarf's problem?"

"Hey, Joey," Sallie tries to make a dent on a very difficult surface, "I am not a shrink ... you are not a shrink. But what I was getting ready to explain to you guys, it is sorta like the Dwarf, or at least the Dwarf's mind, is a prisoner of – well, in this case – Louie the Louse's mother. It could be any mother, because with Donato ... "

But Joey the Clown had already bolted out without even waiting to hear Big Nose Sallie relate Fats' tale to the rest of us.

When Sallie is finished, so is our poker game. At this point, nobody's head is working too good. It is like a story right outta Ripley's "Believe It Or Not" and in this case I think all of us would not, except that is a choice we do not have open to us when Sallie says we all gotta put our heads together and figure out what to do about such a serious situation. I am sure it is a problem we would have solved, but you must take my word for that because we never even get the chance. Instead, we all wind up at Coney Island Hospital the next morning to visit Joey the Clown.

Everybody got their own way of working out a problem. Me, I like the thinking part. When Big Nose Sallie tells us to put our heads together to figure it out – that is my way – I am definitely a thinker. Joey the Clown, on the other hand, is absolutely not a thinker. He is a doer! Maybe much of it is instinct, but I always feel doin' can getcha in a lot more trouble than thinking. For instance, when my old lady squawks, which is pretty often, "Sonny, do this! Sonny, do that!" I always tell her, "I'll think about it! I'll think about it!" And that is exactly what I do, and that is all that I do – which is because I got a head on my shoulders and inside of that head is brains, and I use them. Joey the Clown may also have brains – I do not dispute the fact – but if he does they have a much higher trade-in value than mine because they are virtually unused. Do not misinterpret what I am saying – the world needs guys like Joey and I love him. But the truth happens to be, he is strictly an action guy – a doer. If somebody keeps a scorecard I am sure it would show that doers put in much more Emergency Room time than thinkers.

Anyhow, I get awakened so early in the morning you'd think I was a farmer. There is this knock on the door and Foghorn Manganaro is croakin', "Joey's in the hospital. We're all goin' over there in about ten minutes."

It is such an ungodly hour, my eyes stay stuck closed, they just do not work, but my mouth does. "What's he doin' in the hospital?"

"All I can tell ya is, he ain't a doctor."

Actually, when we get there we find out he ain't much of anything except a pile of bandages. There is no way I know it is the Clown. If you tell me it is Bela Lugosi, maybe I would believe that because what I see through the little window, laying in the bed, is a mummy. But none of us spend much time lookin' through that little window because Goldie, the Clown's girl , is swish-swashin' back 'n forth down the corridor and when Goldie is around you usually are unable to look very much at anything else. I am also now very happy that my eyes are no longer stuck closed. Goldie is constructed in such a way that requires much studious observation and consideration. Looking at her makes you appreciate that when God has the time, he really turns out quality work. I cannot believe that the parts that my Theresa was made with comes from the same factory or parts department as the parts that were used for Goldie, unless maybe Goldie was a special order or somethin'. If ya gonna look for a defective part, you just won't find one, unless maybe your countin' the inside; if you go inside, all the way at the top, there you may find a shortage – probably a rush job on that part. Which may also be the explanation of why such a doll has eyes only for the Clown. Hopefully, this is a slow day at Coney Island Hospital because it is not only our eyes that follow Goldie up and down the corridor, but every nurse, intern and doctor on the floor seem to be doing not much else but examining her like she is gonna be in a medical journal; also, you get the feeling that all the x-ray equipment in this place is imbedded right in the eyeballs of some of these medics.

At this moment the Dwarf gets off the elevator and Goldie, who is snifflin' and sobbin' while everyone is thinking how much they would like to comfort her, turns and starts hip-swishing her way over to him.

The Dwarf is obviously one very upset person right now. Big Nose Sallie asks him, "What took you so long?"

The Dwarf shakes his head. "Aw, I had Widder Brown drive me over and it was a little outta her reign of terror." He turns as he sees Goldie bouncing her way over to him and it looks like she is being followed by Gangbusters as four or five cops who were standing around now come to life. Never have I seen such a hang-dog look on the Boss as he says, "Goldie, believe me, I still do not know what happened, but I am sorry."

Goldie looks up at him and she is crying. "Boy, when you go crazy, you even do that in a very big way. What're you trying to do – make me a widow before I am even a wife?"

"I would never hurt one of my own, Goldie," the Dwarf pleads with his arms outspread, which takes up much of the hospital corridor. "Believe me, I like Joey. And life is too short as it is."

"And you sure do your part to make sure of that, don't you, Mr. Langella?" Goldie snaps with one of her pootey-poo smiles. But before she is able to utter another word she is most rudely interrupted.

"So, first it's McTavish, then it's Otto the Pawnbroker and now Joey DiCollonna. Ya tryin' to catch up to Jack the Ripper, Langella?" It is not Sherlock Holmes and it is not Dick Tracy; it is just one of the Johnny-Come-Latelies from the local precinct who has not yet learned who butters his bread. He is led away quickly and quietly by one of his older, wiser associates who, we assume gives an accelerated course in stepping on toes and scratching backs, which gives Goldie the opportunity to go back on the attack. "I know Joey can sometimes do certain very strange things. Remember, he is under much stress right now as we are discussing the possible impending union of two lives – mine and his, although at this moment we are not too certain of the availability of his, thanks to you. No matter what Joey does, did you have to throw him out the window?" This, I must say, is an attention-getter. We are all now lookin' at the Dwarf like we cannot believe what we just hear. This kinda news we do not wanna wait two days to read in a paper we buy from the Widder Brown.

"I did not throw Joey outta no window, Goldie. He sorta bounced off the wall and it is like a carom shot on his second bounce that he goes out the window. I do not even know it is Joey at this time." It is not too often that either joy or sadness register or anything else regeisters on the Dwarf's face but at this moment, this is the most disconsolate Boss I have ever seen. "Here is this wild man shooting up my cupboard in the middle of the night. What am I supposed to do?"

This rings a bell with one of the cops, who interrupts the Dwarf, "Sounds like the same looney that shot the window out of Mrs. Lee's Chop Suey House over on Neptune Avenue. When the call comes in we think maybe it is a tong war. If it ain't no tong war and it is our boy Joey here, he hadda been on some very heavy stuff." This I do not personally understand because although Mrs. Lee, who is the only Chinese person in our neighborhood, is a very mysterious lady with very little feet, I have never heard anyone say anything bad about her. It is true that if it is the Clown who perpetrates such a deed, rhyme and reason do not necessarily enter into it.

Big Nose Sallie's face is all scrinched up, he is thinkin' so hard. It is like he knows somethin' but he really doesn't quite know it; it is sitting on the tip of his tongue but he just can't spit it out. Goldie's face doesn't scrinch. Her eyes just get bigger and bigger when she does not understand things, and right now nothing that she hears adds up – one and one just does not make two and she feels that even an adding machine will not help her ... or in this case, an abacus. Right in the middle of all the scrinching and eye-popping, Fats gives out a yelp like a puppy whose tail got stepped on and then sinks to the floor as if he is a corkscrew opening a champagne bottle. Such a condition is caused by the emergence of what is obviously Joey the Clown but to a person such as Fats Suozzo, who never misses a Saturday matinee at the movies, when his shoulder is tapped by five-feet-ten inches of bandage it should not be too much of a surprise when he howls, "It is the Mummy's Curse" on his swoon to the floor.

While a whole crowd of people in white gowns run up and are all trying to lift Fats onto a gurney, which is no easy job for a bunch of outta shape kids fresh out of medical school, the bandaged head is going, "Ooh, Goldie! I gotta go real bad an' I cannot find no flap or nothin'." As no mummy would ever have such a problem and as we do not believe there is any mummy that is personally acquainted with Goldie, we are now certain by the process of elimination, that what we are looking at is definitely Joey the Clown.

All it takes is a few slaps in the face and the medical corp is finished with Fats – maybe not in the same league as the cure for polio but, still, another technological achievement for the scientific community – and immediately they are able to turn their attention to Joey, whom they are surrounding with a small arsenal of scissors. Joey, it seems, does not like the area which these scissors are pointing to and again calls out, "Goldie, I don't gotta go so bad anymore." Goldie, who originally comes from Hoboken, which explains her very dainty and delicate nature, does her very best to come to Joey's rescue. "Don't you have any concern for this man's dignity?" But it seems that they were much more concerned with what can possibly happen to their scrubbed and shiny hospital floor as they snicker-snack their way to what can best be described as a certain amount of freedom for Joey; and Goldie, who is suddenly viewing what she did not expect to view before her wedding night, now temporarily replaces Fats on the gurney. Naturally, all the young doctors are very anxious to join in the resuscitation process and show much disappointment when Goldie bounces up by herself before they have a chance to show their stuff.

Originally, the Coney Island police force is here because with the Clown flying out of the Dwarf's window, on top of the old suspicions of the disappearances of Knuckles McTavish and Honest Otto, the order is given to bring the Dwarf in. This does not warm the cockles of any of the hearts resting beneath the badges of the N.Y.P.D. because it seems to be the type of assignment that could have a wide variety of outcomes. So, what they learn just now about the very strange behavior of Joey the Clown makes for a somewhat happier contingent of men in blue. They are now faced with a job action that is very much more to their liking, especially now that it is obvious that Joey the Clown is, somehow, still in one piece. One of the cops – a sergeant – asks the Dwarf, "Is this the guy that shot up your apartment, Mr. Langella?"

It is a grunt, which is the way the Dwarf speaks very often, especially to people who wear badges, "Nobody shot up my apartment – just my cupboard."

When Joey sees the Dwarf, he is shaking so much, it is like his bandages are gonna unwind. "Geez, Donato, ya sure got a funny way of showin' yer appreciation whenever I try to help ya out."

"What kinda help me out?" the Dwarf growls. "You sneak in and shoot up my furniture like a lunatic! Ya call that helpin' me out?"

"So ya gotta throw me out the window? It's lucky I landed on the milkman's horse. I'm tellin' ya, Boss, if Borden's sues me I'm bringin' you inta it."

At which this very sharp-witted sergeant who does a lot of squinting and head-shaking, snaps, "Aha! So you're both admittin' that it was Joseph DiCollonna who perpetrates this act!"

"I think maybe ya oughta shut up, Joey," the Dwarf advises.

"I ain't ashamed of what I did," Joey don't pay no attention to the Dwarf. "I did what any red-blooded American would do if his leader wuz bein' made a monkey of." At this moment it is not necessary that the Boss have a face that smiles or frowns for us to know this is not exactly Happy Hour for him. It is a big plus for Joey that he is in a hospital surrounded by an army of policemen.

"You better believe it," Goldie adds. "Joey stands up all the time for the National Anthem and always takes his hat off – even if it's raining – and he don't even know the words. Blood does not get much redder than that."

"And I suppose you were saving your leader when you shot up Mrs. Lee's Chop Suey House earlier that same evening?", the sergeant bellowed.

It is very difficult watching a pile of bandages say the things that we are hearing now, because we cannot see any expression – we can only imagine what the Clown's face is doing with this conversation. But his mouth is doing okay all by itself. "I ain't no dummy," it says. I am not sure we take this remark at face value. "It is obvious from what Big Nose Sallie tells us that Mrs. Lee has learned many mystical tricks from the Orient ..." We are now hearing words of wisdom from a guy who has sat through more Saturday matinee thrillers, read more comic books and listened to more radio serials than anyone else on this planet with the possible exception of Fats Suozzo.

Again, it is very fortunate that we are in a hospital because now it looks like Big Nose Sallie is having a stroke. Automatically, I turn around to see if the much-used gurney is still there. "He is already in a strait-jacket," Sallie roars. "Now all he needs is a padded cell. I never said nothin' of the sort. I'm tellin' ya, he landed on his head, not on a horse."

"Ya shouldn't oughta call me a liar, Salvatore," the Clown sounds very wounded. "I am not sayin' anything bad about you – even though you or none of the other guys would help out our Boss. Didn't ya say to all of us that Mrs. Lee was able to change herself into Louie the Louses's mother?"

"What're ya talkin' about?" Sallie was so mad, he was sputterin' now.

"I told ya, I ain't no dummy. I saw enough Fu ManChu movies with Goldie an' heard enough "Shadow" programs on the radio to learn all about these Oriental mind tricks. I still don't figure out how Louie the Louse gets a Chinese mother but I am sure it is one of these cloudin' the mind tricks. Ya told us that Louie's mother took over Donato's mind and I wuz able to put two an' two together when ya said that the boss couldn't do anything about Louie because there wuz a chink in his armoire. And we all know the only Chinese person around here is Mrs. Lee ... "

"What kind of talk is this ... I never said anything about no one hiding in no armoire or cupboard or nothin'," Sallie wuz screamin' now. "Ya oughta be ashamed of yourself, you dirty lowlife! Why are you trying to lay this off on me?"

Fats taps Sallie on the shoulder and it looks like Sallie is gonna eat him up. "Excuse me, Salvatore," whispers a very frightened Fats. "I think Joey is referrin' to when ya said that the Boss has a chink in his armor."

"That is exactly what I said ya said, Sallie ... 'The Boss has a chink in his armoire', and you had previously just finished tellin' us that this chink in the Boss's armoire wuz also cloudin' the Boss's mind and wuz Louie the Louse's mother. So when I saw you guys weren't gonna do anything about savin' the Boss I went an' did it by myself – and I only hope I wuz successful and saved the Boss's mind. "

Big Nose Sallie is just standing there with his mouth hanging open. There is no way speech is gonna come outta that mouth for a while. All the other guys are just standing there, staring at this pile of talking bandages like they cannot believe what they just heard. Goldie has a very strange expression on her face, sorta like "I heard it but that don't mean it was really said." Finally she speaks, and it is in a very soft voice. "You know, sometimes it takes a very long time for history to recognize a truly great deed. And also, maybe Salvatore was a little bit right. I mean, if Joey says he fell on a horse, I'm sure he did. But maybe just an eentsie-peentsie part of his head missed the horse and hit the ground – very hard."

CHAPTER EIGHT

GOLDIE, GERTIE AND CAKE

Due to mitigating circumstances Joey does not go to jail, which makes Goldie very happy. In fact, he does not even go to trial. We are all sitting in the courtroom with boxes of cookies and other little goodies which we think will be very comforting to Joey while he is in the slammer as we are sure that a guy who does what he did will not be given the keys to the city. We do not get a chance to even see or hear Joey because he is first taken into the judge's chambers for what they call a pre-trial conference. We are waiting about fifteen minutes when the door from the judge's chambers opens and first Joey the Clown comes out shrugging his shoulders at us like to say "I don't know what's goin' on." Following right behind him are two court-room officers whose hands are criss-crossed between them forming a seat and sitting in this seat with his head bouncing like it is on a swivel spring and his glasses hanging from one ear, is the judge. He is moving his two hands back and forth like he is conducting some invisible orchestra and is mumbling over and over again what sounds like, "A man flies ... a horse dies ... a cupboard's shot ... Mrs. Lee is not ... a man flies ... a horse dies ... a cupboard's shot ... Mrs. Lee is not ..."

It is very obvious that here is a gentleman who is in most serious need of an extended vacation in the country. We all know that Joey the

Clown is not the easiest person to have a conversation with but we gotta assume it is really the daily stress and strain of his job that removes this judge from his bench. And as it seems no other judge is very anxious to take over and have a talk with Joey he is given his walking papers. However, Joey feels he is still entitled to the cookies we brung to court which he polishes off all by himself even before we get back to the Club.

Until now, Goldie does not hear about the Boss' talk with the tattered waif and how it makes for the wishy-washy way he deals with Louie the Louse. She cannot learn about it from Joey because Joey jumps the gun and leaves the Club before Big Nose Sallie tells of such talk. So, when she hears about it from us in the courtroom, although it still makes no sense to her for Joey doing what he did, at least she knows the reason why. As for the Dwarf, she shows much surprise over his having such a soft spot for mothers. She says the rest of us she can understand behaving in such a way, but in the Dwarf's case she could never even think of him as having a mother. When Fats shoots back, "It is very appropriate behavior that the Boss shows. Every great man in history – they all had mudders. How d'ya think the Boss gets born anyhow?"

Goldie gives him a strange, little look and answers, "I don't know. I guess in his case, an acorn, maybe."

It is the day after the Clown walks outta court a free man that Goldie returns to her job serving cheesecake at Junior's on Flatbush Avenue, which is a big climb in the right direction for a doll from Hoboken. Goldie has already taken off two days from work and is not desirous of losing her spatula to some opportunist from the Salad or Appetizer counter. As Junior's cheesecake is the piece d' resistance for which this establishment is best known it is only natural that to be the person behind the counter in charge of serving up such delicacy is the spot which everyone is shooting for. So that is why Goldie sets up no alliances or friendships in this part of the restaurant. It is like the gunfighter that must always be watching out for every gunslinger that comes along looking to take over his place in the order of things. However, as it is an innermost need of every doll to have someone to share her secrets with and a person with whom she can confide, Goldie has built this friendship with Gertie the cocktail waitress as cocktail waitresses are known to be very happy where they are at and have no big eyes for the cheesecake counter. They are two separate worlds – cocktails and cheesecake do not mix.

When Goldie returns to her job, her head is swimming with what has transpired the past coupla days and she feels like she is gonna bust wide open if she does not get the chance to tell somebody about it. As there is neither a priest nor a confessional box available at this time – Junior's works on a tight budget trying to keep its menu prices competitive – Gertie, although her uniform does not exactly conform to the role, is the confessee by default. This is a role that is interchangable between the two of them according to which chest has to be cleared at which time.

Most confessions generally end with "Hail Marys ..," but when Goldie has to relate something involving Joey, which is almost all the time, she starts off with the "Hail Mary", very softly to herself, because she realizes that Gertie may have some erroneous, preconceived ideas about Joey, even though she has not yet had the pleasure or adventure of meeting him. Much of this notion is probably due to when Goldie first starts working at Junior's and Gertie overhears her talking to the Clown on the phone, giving him directions so he can meet her after work. When she tells him she is working at Junior's he asks where is this place and she tells him it is in Downtown Brooklyn. "Then it must be in the Atlantic Ocean," he points out, "as that is the only place downtown from where I am at, Coney Island."

Goldie is one very patient individual. Dealing with Joey, that is a quality ya gotta have. "Joey, Junior's is not in the Atlantic Ocean and you should understand for any city or town, Downtown is the heart of that place – it is where the action is. It could be North, East, South or West."

"Oh, that is very good, Goldie. I could just see myself gettin' into a cab an' tellin' the hackie, 'Driver, go North, East, South or West. I gotta pick up my girl.' I mean, maybe this hackie got a little spinner in his glove compartment an' this spinner just so happens to have all the directions on it an' he gives a spin an' whatever it lands on – that is where I go. If you can wait in front of Junior's a coupla hundred years, I am sure I will pick you up."

"That is a very good idea, Joey." Goldie is still tryin' very hard not to be exasperated, especially since Gertie is now stopped dead in her tracks, drinking up this conversation like it is the trayful of martinis she is balancing on her hand and it looks like it is having the same effect on her. "Just get in a cab," then she turns away from the phone and smiles at Gertie - "He has such a quick mind." - "Just get in a cab and tell the cabdriver to take you to Junior's. Any cabbie will know where it is."

"Is it more'n two blocks from the Surf Avenue subway?" Joey asks.

"Of course it is."

"Then I really cannot do that," Joey apologizes.

"What do you mean you can't do it?" Goldie's voice is definitely at a higher pitch now.

"Ya know, I got this allegiance to the Widder Brown," he explains, "An' it is obviously outta her allowable range ..."

It is quite a while that Goldie is the cheesecake girl at Junior's now and still the Clown has not been able to navigate his way to get there. Fats Suozzo thinks this is very natural as he is convinced, even though nobody listens to him, that Joey DiCollonna is a direct decendant of Christopher Columbus and suffers the same problem – he gets lost with directions – Chris, Fats feels he can call him that as he is family, could never find his way to India for spices and gold and Joey cannot find his way to Junior's for cheesecake and Goldie.

That is why Goldie feels Gertie has certain preconceived ideas about Joey and why she has to start off very carefully whenever she is talking about him. Goldie accepts Joey for the person he is but she realizes that there probably is not another person on this entire planet who can do likewise. Many people cannot understand how a doll such as Goldie, whose curves are much more dangerous than the curves on the Palisades Interstate Parkway going through Bear Mountain, is the way she is about the Clown. Ya gotta understand the person Goldie is. All her grown-up life whenever a guy looks at her, his hands go to work before his mouth can say 'Hello', which makes Goldie one very defensive-minded young lady. So it is quite a different feeling she gets when she first meets the Clown, which is sort of a coming out party for Goldie – coming outta a whipped cream cake, that is. It is a few years ago that the Dwarf throws this big victory celebration block party when Japan throws in the towel and World War Two is over. The centerpiece of this party is a giant-sized red, white 'n blue whipped cream cake which, while the band is playin' "Yankee Doodle", the top pops up and out steps Goldie, who at this time in her life is hired out to step outta cakes all over New York and New Jersey for weddings, confirmations, bar mitzvahs and smokers. It is not a job she loves because as soon as she emerges from inside the cake all the hands around the table start swiping at her like she is a loose gob of whipped cream, there to be devoured. Only this time it is different. As soon as she rises outta the cake the first thing she sees is the face of Joey the Clown. To some people this could be a very frightening experience as no two things on the Clown's face match, but what Goldie sees is a look of such desire and yearning – it is almost a look of hunger – a look of pleading, as if to say 'let this be mine' – she feels protected and comfortable. No one ever looks at her in such a way before. It is like everyone around the table is affected by how the Clown is acting; as he comes closer and closer and his eyes grow wider and, it seems a little misty, everyone else starts backing off and all the reaching, groping hands fade away. What Goldie never, never realizes – you gotta know the Clown to understand – is that what makes him behave in such an emotional, loving, craving way ...is the cake ... that is just the way the Clown is ... but, anyhow, that is why Goldie, since that day, only has eyes for the Clown.

So, when Goldie starts telling Gertie what transpires in her life the past couple of days she does so very carefully, adding a little here, leaving out a little there, realizing that someone could get a very improper inpression of her Joey if it is not told in the right way. She does not pass along any untruths; let us just say she abridges a bit. What comes through to Gertie is this unbelievable display of loyalty and devotion shown by Goldie's boy friend to his Boss where he is pitted against foreign intrigues and even supernatural forces. She is most impressed at the part where he flies out the window – Goldie does a very quick job of glossing over that – and she is wondering if maybe her friend Goldie is in the same class as Lois Lane.

It is only because Gertie's mind is so inquisitive that she wants to know what kinda boss does Joey have and how does he get in such a pickle to begin with that Goldie tells Fats' version of the Dwarf's encounter with the tattered waif, but does not get very far at all. "It is that Joey's boss, the Dwarf, is deceived and maybe even hypnotized by this nymph sent by one, Louie the Louse ..."

"Hold on, Sweetie," blurts a suddenly bug-eyed, drop-jawed Gertie. "Waif ... not nymph – got it? Terminology is most important. It is a waif, not a nymph." The two of them just stand there, staring each other in the eye, neither believing what is coming outta the other's mouth.

CHAPTER NINE

THE UNMASKING

Everyone is pretty comfortable hunkering around the Club later that evening. Some of us are sitting at the table playing poker. Big Nose Sallie and Vito "The Fuse" Fusillo are sitting on stools at the counter reading the early edition of the Daily News to check the results at Belmont. Fats Suozzo and Vito's nephew, Bennie DeLuca, are sitting on the big, cushiony sofa by the pool table eating Mallomars and reading the funnies, explaining to each other what the other one does not understand – L'il Abner can get pretty confusing. And Goldie is sitting on Gertie, who is not quite as comfortable as the sofa but, on the other hand, is a lot more comfortable than the stools. Also, Gertie is not too pleased being a piece of furniture but at this time Goldie is a doll possessed, waiting for the Dwarf, who has not yet arrived. It is not that Goldie does not have a deep fondness for Gertie, whom she admires and respects very much, but she has just found out that her closest friend may be the Brooklyn equivalent of Axis Sally and Tokyo Rose.

Gertie tries very hard to explain that it is because of the Show Business that flows through her veins that she is in such a predicament. The truth is, Gertie, who was known in the Flatbush 'Thee-ayter' as 'Gertie Gutenyu from Flatbush Avenoo', coulda been tried and convicted as a co-conspirator to murder for the death of Vaudeville. In her defense it could be said that certain of her talents brought to mind some of the greats of the theater – when she tap-danced you would think of Charlie Chaplin, when she sang, it was Jerry Collonna – and when she acted she would have her audience rolling in the aisles, their sides splitting with laughter – only she would be doing a Shakespearean tragedy like MacBeth.

When Goldie first starts working at Junior's she holds Gertie Gutenyu in great awe as never before has she been in personal contact with a living, breathing legend of Show Business which Gertie is, having her picture in the Brooklyn Eagle on four separate occassions, although one, maybe, should be discounted as it is a picture of her getting water pumped outta her after falling outta a rowboat on Prospect Park Lake. She has a peaches and cream complexion, although there is an occassional strawberry thrown in here 'n there, and on top of her head, there is like a jungle of rusty bedsprings bouncing around every which way. Her features are not dainty like Goldie's but all-in-all she is not uninteresting to look at. As far as her figure goes, she would do herself a big favor not hanging around too close to Goldie, but that sorta advice goes for just about anyone. Junior's, she explains to Goldie, is a temporary stop-over on her climb to stardom. After all, if Lana Turner gets discovered in a drug store, isn't it good logic, that she, Gertie Gutenyu, will be an even bigger discovery as Junior's is certainly larger and more impressive than any drug store.

It is two minutes to eight that night when the whole world stops turning, there is no longer any movement – even the hands of the clock on the wall just freeze – when the Dwarf comes in and sees what Goldie is sitting on. The only sound that is heard is a very soft, "Five'll getcha ten Goldie's gonna haveta find a new seat."

I am not too sure what we really expected to happen; maybe it is just that we got wild imaginations. After all, ain't the Dwarf still believing that this here Gertie who is being sat on by Goldie - it should only happen to me - is a poor, lost child of the street taken in and cared for by Louie the Louse? No matter, we sit there, frozen in whatever position we were in when the Dwarf first comes through the door, just like those giant dinosaurs they find inside of icebergs, waiting for whatever is gonna happen, to happen.

The Dwarf does not say a word. He looks around the room – it is like he is in a museum surrounded by statues – then walks behind the counter to the espresso machine and pours himself a steaming cup of coffee, turns to Big Nose Sallie, "We got some new furniture, Salvatore?", and his eyes move across to Goldie and Gertie. This immediately melts the iceberg and there is once again motion and sound in the world.

Fats nudges Bennie DeLuca and giggles very softly, "Can't the Boss just kill ya, Bennie?"

Bennie gulps and whispers back, "Anyone ever tell ya, you got a very poor way of expressin' yerself, Fats!" Meanwhile Sallie, who is not having one of his fast days, asks, "What is this about new furniture, Donato?"

"You mean to tell me, what Goldie is sittin' on ain't a couch, ya know – one of them new, contemporary styles?" The Boss says this with a straight face, which is the way the Boss says everything, so it neither throws us off nor gives us a hint if what he is saying he really means. But I think we can safely assume that in the Dwarf's mind he is being a top banana right now.

"Yoo-hoo," Gertie gives a half-wave by wiggling the fingers on her left hand and shrugging with a silly little grin at the Dwarf from her pinned-down position on the floor. "It's me again ... I am back ... and I am not a couch ... and I think you know that."

"I can tell you are not a couch because a couch would have a longer skirt than you do." It is true that Gertie is not dressed in what one would call formal attire as she is still wearing her tu-tu style cocktail waitress' uniform because Goldie did not even give her time to change. Goldie, maybe because she has just discovered she is not sitting on a couch, but more probably because she realizes that escape for Gertie now, is impossible, stands up, allowing Gertie to do the same. The Dwarf continues, and it sounds to me like his voice is much more serious, "I hope you are not here to bring me bad news about Louie's mother. For her I wish only peace and good health. But I am beginning to get a very funny feeling. Seeing you this way instead of the rags you were wearin' then ... it makes you look like a completely different kind of person ... and it makes me think maybe I am goin' to hear some very interesting things ... after which you again may be dressed differently – like in a shroud." We are then able to get in about ten hands of poker, which is about thirty minutes, as that is how long it takes Goldie, Big Nose Sallie and Vito to revive Gertie. Goldie is really not too much help as she is the whole time giving the Boss a what's-for, telling him how much courage Gertie had coming here, and that she never woulda had Gertie come here if she had any idea he was gonna act this way.

It is hard to tell, but you get the feeling that the Dwarf is a little bit on the defensive. "You just ain't got no sense of humor, Goldie. I was only bein' funny, but you don't know a joke when you hear one."

Goldie looks way up in his eyes and for a long minute does not answer at all, then she finally shrugs and asks him, "You got a nickel you can lend me?"

This change of conversation catches the Dwarf off-guard but he reaches in his pocket, pulls out some coins and says, "Here, it ain't a loan. I can afford to give you a nickel, but what the heck do ya need it for?"

"Oh, I just want to call Bob Hope and let him know he better watch out. There is this comedian from Coney Island breathing down his back."

It was probably never known outside of the Mermaid Social Athletic Club that if that night the Dwarf was not a man of honor and does not control his temper, there would be about a dozen less mothers shopping in Coney Island the next day and every day after that, for that matter. Because that is how many mothers had their lives sworn on by their sons to assure Gertie that no harm comes to her before she agrees to continue with her confession, which follows right after Goldie lets it be known that she is no bounty hunter.

"My friend and co-worker, Gertie, whom many of you I am sure recognize as a star of stage and screen, is here of her own choice and free will ..."

"Oh, so I guess the two of ya take turns sittin' on each other, then." It is Foghorn Manganaro questioning the veracity of Goldie's statement, which Goldie ignores like it was completely unheard, an occurrence that cannot happen when Foghorn speaks even if you are born with two tin ears.

"The strangest thing happens," Goldie continues, "when I am relating certain things that Joey does."

"It would be strange if strange things didn't happen when it comes to what the Clown does," Vito Fusillo throws his two cents in.

With her hands on her hips, Goldie gives us that real pouty look and thrusts out her chest, which she knows will get her our undivided attention, and says, "I will simply ignore all ignorant remarks, which means I will have to pay attention to nothing that you might say." If she is waiting for applause or some kinda standing ovation, she is one very disappointed doll. "Like I was saying, it is the strangest feeling to tell someone what you consider a deep, dark secret, only to have that someone not just tell you it is their deep, dark secret also, but to actually know more about it than you do. And that is exactly what happens when I tell my dear friend Gertie of Joey's courage and loyalty in defending Mr. Langella. In order to explain why Mr. Donato Langella needs such defending I, naturally, describe his meeting with this poorly dressed nymph ..."

"Waif! It was a meeting with a tattered waif!" Gertie is most huffy as she corrects Goldie. "There is no nymph." She then steps from behind Goldie where she has sorta been hiding since she stops being a couch and walks to the center of the room and waits for a minute until everyone is looking at her. Then she spreads her arms out with her palms up to the ceiling like she is balancing two trays of martinis and says, "Gentlemen, let me explain something. I am a thespian." All at once, everybody in the room suddenly has to clear his throat and we are all looking down to see if maybe our shoelaces are untied. Nobody is looking at anybody else and, certainly, nobody is able to look at Gertie until Big Nose Sallie, whose throat is obviously still giving him some discomfort gives a big double "Ahem! Ahem!" and still checking his shoelaces while he is talking, says, "Maybe some people find it hard to believe, but we are basically a pretty open-minded bunch of guys. Also, it is really not necessary for you to go into your personal, private life." Sallie cannot help it when he finishes with a very quiet, "Tsk! Tsk! What a shame."

Gertie cannot understand what is transpiring. She is feeling like a foreign flick with no sub-titles, but a good trouper gotta go on, so she explains how, because Show Business is in her blood, she goes to the Actors' Studio three times a week for lessons. It is there that she has the very good fortune, in her mind, to be discovered by an agent on the sidewalk right in front of the studio. "It is amazing, but just by looking at me he recognizes that I am an actress. I have seen him in front of the studio many times – I could not forget him with that red plaid vest he wears – it is sort of his trademark. And he is always with a great big smile on his face." Everybody's head is nodding up an' down as we now become a choral speaking group, all reciting at the same time, "Louie the Louse!"

"What makes ya think this bum is any kind of agent?" Vito asks.

"How could you doubt it?" Gertie is really shocked at such a question. "He recognizes my talent immediately. And he is so giving of himself ..."

"He oughta be," the Dwarf mutters. "There ain't a single part of him worth a plugged nickel."

"You may not believe it," Gertie goes on, "because such generosity is unheard of in his field; he actually accepts me as a client and is so confident of my success that rather than have me face the burden of having to pay him his ten per cent in one lump sum when he lands me my first role, he permits me to start paying him immediately twenty-five dollars each week towards his fee. And, get this, if I want to pay more than twenty-five, he is willing to accept it. What do you think about that?"

The Dwarf, he just nods his head and grunts, "Now I can understand why you call this man a saint."

Vito, who we all know, is one very sharp businessman, is finding it very difficult to swallow this. "I dunno, Gertie. You don't check this guy out at all? When I go to Belmont I get a Form Sheet that tells me everything I wanna know about a nag before I plunk my dough down on it. Don't you check out a Form Sheet or references before plunking down money on such a guy?"

"Oh, he has very strong credentials," Gertie assures us. "He told me that he was even involved in 'Gone With The Wind'."

"The only thing he is involved with that is gone with the wind are the numbers slips that belonged to me," the Dwarf throws in. "But enough of this baloney. Let us get down to brass tacks, Little Miss Marker."

"No! No!" Gertie is almost in a panic as she corrects the Dwarf. "That is Shirley Temple. I know, it is so easy to mix us up – but, if you look closely, her hair is a little blonder than mine."

"I promise, I will never mix you up again. But like I was sayin', let us get down to brass tacks. Is Louie really takin' care of his sick mother? And if he is so good and generous to ya, how come you was walkin' around dressed like a rag-picker?"

"Try to put yourself in my place," Gertie starts, wringin' her hands while she talks.

"It is impossible. The Boss could not fit," Fats points out, always very quick on the uptake and equally as quick to help out.

"What I mean," Gertie goes on, "is that Louis, my agent, is a very persuasive and a very charming gentleman."

The Dwarf turns to the rest of us, "Believe it or not, I have shown her the picture of Louie – you know – the one that was hangin' in the Post Office and she says it is definitely the same 'charming gentleman' whom she calls Louis," at which point he turns back to Gertie, "but I am still waiting to hear about how Louie takes care of his poor, sickly mother and if it is so it is certainly a most virtuous as well as a redeem-ing quality which makes such a person deserving of reconsideration of his life-span."

"It is not a simple 'Yes', 'No' answer," Gertie is wailing and looking to Goldie for help.

The Boss shows to me he would be a very easy-going teacher, "Then I will make it Multiple Choice. A - Louie takes care of his poor, sickly mother; B - Louie does not take care of his poor, sickly mother; C - The bum does not even have a mother; or, D - None of the above. And if ya choose 'None of the above' it immediately becomes an essay answer. Please, for your own sake and health, do not fail this test."

Gertie is not prepared for this test as she is blubbering like a colicky baby but Goldie is like the whole Apache nation on the warpath after raiding the outpost's liquor store right outta a John Wayne western. The Dwarf is in no danger of being scalped as it is totally outta reach but his shins look like they may be in a lotta trouble right now.

"Did anyone ever tell you that you are a big bully?"

"Well, let me put it this way," the Dwarf answers, actually backing off a couple of steps like he doesn't know what is coming at him – a buzzsaw or a locomotive, "nobody ever calls me a little bully."

"You cannot just go around scaring people, dumping them in rivers and throwing them out of windows." It is like there is a Fourth of July fireworks display going on in Goldie's eyes. "Do you know what such behavior leads to?"

"Less people?

"Ooh, you make me so mad!" she hisses, stamping her foot. "How dare you threaten Gertie and make her cry!"

"All I tell her is to prepare for a test so she does not fail." The Boss acts very surprised at Goldie's attitude. "She sure musta upchucked a lotta lunches when she went to school."

"It is all right, Goldie," Gertie sniffles. "He will just have to understand that I cannot answer that question. You see, Mr. Langella, I do not know anything about anybody's mother. It was strictly show biz. I was just following a script prepared by my agent, Louis, and I had to ad-lib when the story-line changes in mid-stream. Louis explains to me that he has a partner, whom happens to be you, and that he is much more of a humanitarian than his partner. He tells me how, because he uses the business' money for good causes you are so angry that he is afraid for his life. Meantime, he is preparing me for a major role on the stage at the Flatbush Theater if I can pass my big audition, which is you."

"I bet if he tells you that the Earth is flat you would not go out in a rowboat in case you go over the edge of the world."

"Oh, I would never go out in a rowboat, no matter what," Gertie says with a gasp. "I once almost drowned in Prospect Park Lake falling out of a rowboat. But, anyhow, for my audition I must convince you to leave your partner Louis alone, and to do that he teaches me the Abraham Lincoln Philosophy of Method Acting."

"The Abraham Lincoln Philosophy of Method Acting?" We are all taking note of the fact that there is now much movement of the Boss' face as he asks this question. Also, he picks up from the pool table a couple of balls which he rolls around in the palm of his hand just as I would do with marbles if I was nervous, a most unusual way for the Boss to act.

"That is correct," Gertie assures us. "He teaches me to say anything convicingly with a straight face and much drama and emotion based on the philosophy of the sixteenth President of the United States – 'You can fool some of the people all of the time, all of the people some of the time, but to be a great actor or actress you've got to be able to fool everybody whenever you want."

"Lincoln said that?" Obviously this did not sound too familiar to the Dwarf.

"Oh, yes." Gertie says this with much conviction. "Louis explains to me that Lincoln was a great devotee of the theater. Do you know that his very last night was spent in the theater. Louis said that the theater was in his blood."

"I think the way it turns out," the Dwarf adds, "it was more like his blood was in the theater, unfortunately. But I think what I am gettin' from the drift of your conversation is that the whole story you tell me as the tattered waif, includin' the part about a sick mother is all made up – it was just play-acting."

Gertie is now very nervous. "It is Show Business, Mr. Langella. It is what I consider my big chance. The whole plot and the role of the tattered waif – it is all my creative ability. I am only sorry that I cannot locate my agent, Louis, since then – he must be out of town on a very big project. Also, you two should kiss and make up and resume your partnership. And please remember – it was not a personal thing at all. I did not even know you, and except for Goldie telling me about her boy-friend ..."

"Yeah! Yeah!" the Dwarf brushes it aside. "No hard feelin's." Never would any of us have believed that the Dwarf could show such charity after he takes this kinda bamboozling and is made to look almost like a human being. "And to show ya my heart is in the right place," he turns around and motions to Fats, "Fats, Gertie has spent a long time here an' she must be very hungry. I want ya to treat her real good and take her to Nathan's an' work around the whole counter – you know – start at the end with the hot dogs ..."

"No, Boss," Fats interrupts with great patience,"the hot dogs are not at the end. First is the pizza, then the hot dogs, then the roast beef, next the chow mein sandwiches..."

"Oh, no. That is okay, really," Gertie pleads, "it is not necessary ..."

"I will not take 'No' for an answer. Fats is the house expert on Nathan's. Remember, Fats, nothin' is to be left out or spared." The Dwarf hands Fats a couple of bills and Fats is in heaven as he starts to leave with a most reluctant Gertie. What Gertie does not hear is what the Dwarf says very quietly to Fats as he hands him the bills – "Finish it up with a double custard and an extra large milk shake and then show her a real good time by takin' her on the Cyclone and I want you to ride that roller coaster all night if ya can. After that, you send her home in a style befittin' such a lady. Put her in the Widder Brown's cab for her ride to the subway. That is what we will call the coup d' grace."

Fats looks at the Dwarf in awe. "How can ya be so good to someone who pulled on ya what she did? How can one person be so forgiving?" And we are all in quiet agreement with Fats, wondering how the Boss stays so calm and benevolent in such a situation.

It is only the next morning when Foghorn and Vito decide to shoot a game of pool and find the eight ball and cue ball crunched all outta shape, almost into powder, that it is figured maybe the Boss was not so calm after all.

CHAPTER TEN

THE LOTTERY

What happens to the Dwarf after our little talk with Gertie and Goldie is not too different from what happens to Popeye whenever an extra-large can of spinach is dumped down his gullet; something like watching an inner tube pumped up by an air hose. It is once again the Dwarf we are used to seeing and all I know is I am now very happy to be a guy named Sonny who is very careful not to go around stepping on toes rather than to be Louie the Louse. We are all very much aware that the Boss will not advertise how he feels about buying Louie's sob story; in fact it is a story which, after a while, he says never happened but it is a figment of our imaginations probably brought on by consuming a batch of over-fermented chianti which was left sitting too long in one of our bath tubs. Nobody contradicts him.

Nobody contradicts him but everybody is holding court. On one side of the room is Fats Suozzo, who looks very carefully first from the corner of one eye, then the corner of the other eye to make sure the Dwarf is nowhere around before he goes into his song and dance which is now beginning to sound like a broken record, "I am not the kinda person who says 'I told ya so but if Donato-baby ,'" (and this from a guy who always calls him the Boss and bows, at least as much as his stomach will permit him), "listens to me in the first place he never woulda been in such a fix. I know all along this doll, this tattered waif or Gertie or whatever she calls herself, is from Hoodwinksville an' I do everything but hit him over the head to tell him. My momma always told me – 'If-a you gonna listen to a woman at all, make-a sure she's-a your mother.' "

On the other side of the room is the Clown and he doesn't care who is around to hear him recite his version of how it is because of him that the Dwarf and his mind are saved. Probably he has already forgotten how he goes flying outta the Dwarf's window or maybe the thought of possibly repeating that trip outta the window of the Mermaid S.A.C. does not upset him that much as it is on the ground level. The rest of us, we do whatever we can to get through this very trying period – like we put cotton plugs in our ears, or we turn up the juke box very loud. Being that it is June, we even try to escape by going to the beach which is only two blocks away, but none of us have a love affair with sand or sun and the water in the ocean is soakin' wet so we just make the best of it hangin' out in the Club. Sometimes we take some ante money outta the pot in our poker game to give to Fats so he can go to a movie. He is not too difficult. With the Clown it is different and we just hope we do not have to wait for old age to solve our problem – it does not matter whose old age, ours or his.

All this is just garnish on the entree; the real belly-bubbler here is waiting to see what is gonna happen – and also how and when – now that the Dwarf is outta his trance and knows that he is made to look like an organ grinder's monkey – or considering it is the Dwarf, an organ grinder's baboon – by Louie the Louse. It is the sort of excitement I do not need in my life, especially since I do not look forward to gettin' an ulcer, which will cause me to have to drink much milk, a fate I would absolutely be unable to handle. To me, it is an unmentionable. In fact, if an emergency arises and my old lady, Theresa, catches me in the right mood, like after a double helping of her zabaglione, and sends me to the grocery because there is nothin' in the fridge for the kids she knows to write on the list 'm–k'. But as I am in the same boat as the rest of the guys, there is nothing we can do except sit back and wait – a most unhealthy situation that makes us unable to attend to business as usual.

We cannot give full concentration at the poker table; the felt top on the pool table gets ripped when Bennie DeLuca, who is known as the Willie Hoppe of Coney Island, has the cue stick slip outta his hands because he keeps his eyes on the Dwarf instead of the pool table and the older guys who come to the Club every day to play bocci out in the back stop playin' and just sit around and watch and wait and wait and watch for whatever is goin' to happen, to happen. We all know that inside the Dwarf there is a storm brewin' right now – maybe even a hurricane – only with the Dwarf you do not get any weather report – the face does not move.

It is only because the Boss knows it is like there is a spotlight shining on him that he does not just go out and do what everyone knows he's gonna do. A short time after Gertie sings her song about Louie being a motherless child the Dwarf learns from Big Nose Sallie who learns from Walter Winchell – not the Walter Winchell who talks to Mr. and Mrs. North America and all the ships at sea – it is our name for one of the friendly boys in blue who broadcasts to us all the interesting tidbits from the local precinct – that someone keeps pointing the finger at the Boss whenever anything happens so he should be very careful. It happens when Knuckles McTavish disappears. It happens when Honest Otto the Pawnproker disappears. It happens whenever there is a situation that involves someone that is in someway associated with the Dwarf. For instance, Winchell explains that when McTavish becomes like the rabbit that the magician puts in a hat and-poof-he is gone, there is this tip phoned into the stationhouse from someone who calls himself "a concerned citizen" with the word that the Dwarf converts McTavish into the cornerstone of a new office building. When "concerned citizen" is told that there must be a name involved to make an official complaint he tells them he is John Smith which the Desk sergeant finds difficult to spell but when he asks Mr. Smith to spell his name they are already cut off.

And when Otto the Honest Pawnbroker does his off-to-Buffalo there is another hot tip called into the stationhouse, this one from "an outraged taxpayer" who, when asked his name, is Joe Jones. Now, the Smiths and the Joneses may thrive and prosper in many parts of our country but in Coney Island and its surrounding suburbs a name usually has a healthy number of syllables to give it body and substance so even though these calls are looked into and that is why all eyes are following the Dwarf, and our Club is sometimes swarming with more cops than our Monday morning cannoli drop-off by Vito can accomodate, there are still some very strong doubts among the local gendarmes, especially those most familiar with the Dwarf. That is why on the next occassion that circumstances bring about another call, which is when the Clown takes his solo flight outta the Dwarf's window, there is a plan of action mapped out. This tip is phoned in by a "fearful resident" who is kept on the line by a very slow-writing sergeant with a broken pencil who needs much assistance in the spelling of each word. During the course of transcribing this tip they are able to trace the call to a phone booth on Surf Avenue just outside the Salt Water Taffy Shop by the subway. The call goes out to their nearest car, which, it seems is being driven by one of the truly superior intellects of this precinct. He reports back that when he approaches the phone booth there is someone in there talking so he asks him, "Are you the 'fearful resident'?" to which the telephone talker immediately responds, "No, the 'fearful resident' just left a minute ago," and he hightails it to the subway and disappears. This crimebuster does not get promoted from this report – but he does make mention that this guy in the phone booth was wearing a red plaid vest like he never saw before. So, with all this attention focused on him, that is why the Dwarf must be very careful about when and how he makes his move.

It happens during one of the poker games from which I had already departed shortly after the appearance of Fivel Finnegan, and I cannot say I am sorry I was not there. The Dwarf does not join in our poker games. He is sitting at a corner table with Big Nose Sallie reading the Racing Form and drinking espresso when a group of four or five local shopkeepers walk in to register a complaint. I am not there but I am told they are shaking so much that it looks like a home movie where the film comes off the reel. Finally, they let it be known that they think it is very unfair to charge them for a neighborhood upkeep insurance policy.

Now, it is true that many years ago, before the Dwarf becomes the Boss, collecting insurance to protect the store owners was not unheard of; and everyone knew what and who they were being protected from. But the Dwarf does very nicely with his various enterprises and looks after his neighbors just because they are his neighbors and they respect him so it is only natural that he is more than just a little surprised at this complaint and asks for a slightly more detailed description of what takes place. It is Giuseppe the Butcher who tells the Dwarf how his assistant, the one who always wears the red plaid vest, makes the rounds of the stores an' tells them that his Boss – Donato Langella – is very concerned for their safety as the neighborhood is going way downhill so his Boss has decided to take matters into his own hands but will have to tax each store owner for this service. Nobody is too happy about this, Giuseppe explains; it is only out of respect for Donato that they all go along, even though many of them could not afford it. But when the one in the red plaid vest comes back a few days later to collect money for a snow removal fund in June they thought maybe it would not be a bad idea if they came in to discuss with Donato the fact that there is a really good chance that it would not snow in June and even if it did, maybe they can shovel their own snow just like they do in the winter. They tell the Dwarf that they already explain this to the one in the red plaid vest and he says that if it does not snow the money will be in what is called a slush fund.

I am told that the Dwarf just stands there but it is like the beginning of an earthquake – as none of the guys have ever sat through a real, live earthquake, maybe this is worse – the whole room is rumbling and shaking so bad that the poker table begins bouncing and all the money starts going like Mexican jumping beans. The group of shopkeepers are clutching at each other for dear life thinking maybe Giuseppe goes a little too far to get the Dwarf this upset. But although the Dwarf seems ready to explode maybe this is the door-opener he needs. He tells Giuseppe that when Louie comes back he should just say to him that Donato Langella provides all the protection for the shopkeepers, and that Donato wants Louie to report to him to clear up this misunderstanding.

Giuseppe is so overcome with gratitude and relief that when he finishes kissing both hands and then the feet of the Dwarf he promises to bring him enough of the choicest cuts of steak to fill up his belly for a year. Fats Suozzo almost faints from envy and Joey the Clown figures to keep such a promise Giuseppe would have to own all the cows in Texas, Oklahoma and maybe even part of Kansas.

Hopefully, the Dwarf does not work up his appetite waiting for such a happening because it is just three days later, when I am sitting in at one of our poker games, that Joey the Clown walks into the Club dangling a toothpick from his lower lip and announces, "Boss, I hope ya like your steaks well-done, I mean very well done." He goes on to explain how he got into the Widder Brown's cab and, as sometimes happens, he tells her to turn in the wrong direction and they wind up in front of Giuseppe's Salumeria or, at least, what used to be Giuseppe's Salumeria or Butcher Shop. Now it was one very big pile of ashes that smells like Peter Luger's Steak House. The Clown goes on to tell how, when he sees Giuseppe sitting at the curb, with his head in his hands, wailing, he walks over and talks to him. Giuseppe cries that when Louie comes back the day after his talk with Donato, he tells Louie exactly what the Boss told him to say and Louie just goes, "Donato knows I do not have the time for these social amenities as I am much taken up with carin' for my ailing mother. If he is of the opinion that a misunderstanding exists, who am I to say it does not. But just in case some unforseen accident occurs, which can happen because Donato Langella is not the accident preventer he is cracked up to be ... and that is why I am now separatin' myself from him ... remember, he is no longer the only game in town. I will be at your service. Naturally, the rates will be somewhat higher once you are known to be accident-prone, but like the French say – save la fee." Then Giuseppe goes on to tell the Clown how he and the other shopkeepers can't afford to have such things happen to them and they probably will be forced to do business with Louie because, so far, Donato does not protect them like he says.

I recognize that I am not playing exactly at my best level when I fold with Aces over Ladies so I must suppose that my head is in a different place, which it is. It is following my ears which are paying very close attention to the Dwarf, which is what my eyes would like to be doing also, but they are afraid so they do not look at him at all; what they are doin', I do not know because I can assure you that they are not looking at the cards either.

The Dwarf, right now, is reminding me of the Big, Bad Wolf gettin ready to blow down a piggy's house. He is huffing an' puffing when he says to Big Nose Sallie, "You will call Squinty DiPalma and tell him I need a couple of his Philadelphia hotshots for an erasing job." It is the kind of a moment where common sense tells you to keep very quiet ... it is no time for speechifyin' or commenting – or anything. Invisible and dumb would be good – and I am working on such a condition when it happens.

"Philly, Shmilly. Five'll getcha ten any guy in this room can take down Louie the Louse." No, Fivel, I thought to myself. You did not say it. I was imagining it. Unfortunately, I do not have a very strong imagination. He was just sitting at the table, concentrating on his cards and puffing on a cigar. I do not believe he really knew he said it. It is like Fivel's mouth works by reflex. Suddenly, it is dark and I cannot hardly see my cards. I did not, for more than a minute, think that Fivel's mouth can cause the end of the world but I was not exactly relieved to see that the darkness was caused by the shadow of the Dwarf, who was now hovering over the table.

"So, any guy in this room can take down Louie the Louse, huh?" Although this is not a very catchy question, nobody answers it .. "Okay. I'm gonna give someone the chance to pick up a lotta cabbage. Five'll getcha ten? Let me tell ya how generous I'm gonna be. I'm puttin' up five grand for you as your ante. So, that means it is ten grand for the guy who does the number on Louie. Don't all jump at me at once."

I never saw a tableful of poker players concentrate on their cards like everyone at this table was doing now. Not only was their eyes, mine included, not moving from their cards at all; I do not think anyone was even breathing. It is not that any of us were in disgreement with the Dwarf's determination that Louie the Louse's membership in the

Mermaid S.A.C. should be terminated, as well as his membership on the Planet Earth. Until now we consider Louie the Louse as unwholesome. This graduates him to bad – very bad. So, even though we are in total agreement with the Dwarf and the incentive is a very motivating one, there are no takers; it must be understood that we are guys with very overcrowded agendas...

"I am waiting for a volunteer but I ain't gonna wait much longer." The Dwarf's voice was getting an edge to it now. You could not tell anything by looking at his face, which no one was doing anyhow, but from his tone you knew he was not getting ready to sing "You Are My Sunshine".

The Clown looks up from the table, where he has just joined us after delivering his news to the Dwarf, and he sounds a little bit shaky, which I can understand. "Just ignore that bum Louie. Sometimes ya gotta be a big person, Donato." I interpret this to mean, "Why don'tcha leave us alone?"

"The Boss already is a big person, Joey." Fats Suozzo, who some-times is a very literal person, says very softly, hoping maybe the whole situation will go away. "In fact he is such a big person he probably don't wanna get any bigger because the Boss does not like to stand out too much in a crowd." With which, Fats sneaks a sideway look at the Dwarf, searching for a sign of approval.

"Fats is right, Joey," the Dwarf agrees, "I'm big enough. I do not wish to be any bigger. Now I have two questions for you. Are you old enough? Would you like to get any older?" It is a moment in time when we would all like to be someplace else. It does not matter too much where that someplace else might be; it does not matter if it is a warm place or a cold place, except maybe to Fivel who would never pick a cold place; it only matters that it is someplace else – not here.

But when the Dwarf's voice lifts us all outta our seats we know for sure that we are here. "Well, being that you are all so excited about get-ting your grubby, greedy hands on such a generous payoff, I will have to be very fair about choosing who the lucky guy is." It is very strange, but I do not notice the excitement that the Dwarf is describing. "I think," the Dwarf goes on, "that the only fair thing is to have a lottery so I will now cut up a sheet of paper so that there will be one piece for every person in the Club. I will then proceed to very fairly mark one piece with an 'X' and you will then very fairly draw one piece each and one very, very lucky person will have very fairly drawn the winning 'X'. What could be fairer?"

"It is very fair," echoes Big Nose Sallie, who, naturally, was excused from the drawing. It is just a couple minutes that the Boss is gone and then returns with a hatful of folded squares of paper that he brings right up to the poker table. "Fivel, I do not wish you to strain yourself by reaching across the table," the Dwarf says, "so I will hand you your ballot." With which the Boss extends his hand with the piece of paper towards Fivel, then brings it back and announces, "In fact I will do even more than that. I will unfold it for you." Fivel's mouth is open but a very rare thing occurs – nothing comes out. "Aha! This is your lucky day, Fivel. The other boys don't even get a chance to draw. We have a winner right off the bat." And the Dwarf then holds up the 'X' marked paper for all of us to see.

"I am not sure that is the piece I would have drawn," Fivel gulps. "In fact it is very definite in my mind that it is not the piece."

"A mere technicality."

"I think maybe I should look at the other ballots. Everything was done so much in a rush. There could always be a mistake and because of that someone else could be missin' out."

"Only if someone raises an objection," the Dwarf says. Looking around the table, he asks, "Does anyone object or does anyone think maybe I did something wrong, like know which piece had the 'X' or something else dishonest?" All the heads at the table very quickly wagged sideways.

"Ya know, Boss," at this moment Fivel is not cold; he is sweatin' beads of perspiration the size of bullets, "I am reconsiderin' my original remark and I am admitting that occassionally I do make an error in judgement. Right now I feel very guilty about depriving Squinty DiPalma and his boys from such a payday. It is common knowledge that the standard of living in a burg like Philly does not measure up to the Big Town and as I personally am a very comfortable person with no further material needs, it is only the right thing for me to pass this on to someone much more in need of it than myself."

The Dwarf shakes his head in what I believe was genuine admiration, like he just heard the Gettysburg Address. "I would expect no less from a person as generous and considerate as yourself. But no one is more deserving and you will not be deprived – and that is the final word – the absolute final word. Case closed! Now that the ten G's are as good as in your pocket just understand one thing. You do not have to bring me the head of Louie the Louse on a silver platter but you do have to give me proof positive that the deed is done."

"No problem, Boss," a very unstrung Fivel stammers, not at all believing himself, but knowing it is very good to whistle when you're walking through a graveyard. "Fivel Finnegan only produces good, clean work. But I ain't gonna advertise it in the Daily News. I am a man of my word. A heavy, outta shape guy like Louie the Louse can always trip and fall into a very deep river wearin' a pair of very heavy shoes. If such an occurence takes place, I will certainly inform you of same in full detail. You said yourself, I cannot bring you his head on a silver platter."

"Very well put, Fivel", the Dwarf agrees. "If such is the case, recognizing that Louie's vest is of a very distinctive quality and style you should be most careful that it does not join the soon-to-be departed on his journey. When you put that vest in my hands it will be the same as his head on a silver platter." At that point Fats Suozzo nudges me and whispers, "Look at that, Sonny. The Boss is smilin'."

"Nah," I answered him, squinting to get a good look. "It's your imagination."

CHAPTER ELEVEN

RENDEZVOUS IN CANARSIE

It should not be assumed just because all the boys in the room let out a whoosh of air that could make a zeppelin fly when Fivel draws the 'X' that it was anything more than relief over the fact that we can now go back to our poker game. Maybe some people would erroneously think that maybe there was a certain degree of nervousness or anxiety involved. This does not offend us but we just do not function in such a way. All ya gotta do is ask any of us and we will tell ya so. Even if such a minconstrued idea coulda been the case, and please do not let this statement make ya think it was, it does not take too long for all the boys at the Mermaid S.A.C. to realize that ten G's is not like ragweed – I mean, ya do not sneeze at such a number. Pretty soon everyone is thinkin' that maybe Fivel Finnegan is one lucky guy, but none of us are so greedy an' selfish that we should approach him an' see if he wants a partner to share in such luck. It is a case where we are very much willing to sit back as spectators and watch a buddy grab the brass ring all by himself.

Fivel, like I told ya, is different from us. It appears that he does not truly appreciate the good fortune that is dumped in his lap. For me this is not too bad because Fivel is not spendin' nearly as much time at the Club under which conditions I can relax an' play as much poker in the middle of the summer as I do in the winter when Fivel is in Miami Beach. When Fivel is spotted on occasion, it seems he no longer walks. Instead of walkin' he is now a slinker. He bounces from shadow to shadow an' after every bounce he turns aroun' to check the last shadow he bounced from. His collar is always pulled up an' the brim of his hat is always pulled down now so all ya see that lets ya know it's him is his needle nose leadin' the way. The coupla times he does come to the Club what we see is, the Widder Brown's cab pulls up in front an' no one else is in it except Minnie – like she is drivin' a passengerless car – then the back door opens like by itself an' out pops Fivel just like he was 'The Invisible Man'. Later, the Widder Brown tells us he must not get too much sleep at home because lately he is always layin' on the floor in her cab. She says she does not know whether to charge him taxi rates or hotel rates. Joey the Clown is of the opinion that maybe Fivel got the whole thing wrong an' does not understand that he is the Chaser, not the Chasee an' is under the impression that Louie the Louse is the one who gets the ten G's for doin' an Abra Cadabra on him, instead of vice-versa.

Actually, the fact of the matter is – Fivel is not brimmin' over with confidence. He now has a job for which, in his mind, he may be over-qualified. He is not absolutely certain of this because Fivel never had a job before an' he would like it very much if that situation had never changed. He tells Fats Suozzo that except for his two sisters he was an only child an' was not accustomed to bein' treated the way he was by the Dwarf who had no idea what a sensitive an' caring soul he was. How it comes about that he tells it to Fats is ... it seems that Fats is very seriously engaged in one of his intermittent diets, this one inspired by the two hours it takes the BMT people to unwedge him from a turnstile, which upsets the Widder Brown very much because she says if she can drive her cab outta the neighborhood, poor Fats would not have suf-fered such an indignity as he would be usin' her cab instead of the BMT an' maybe she should consider makin' longer runs. It is Joey the Clown who leads us, most vigorously, in assurin' her that such is not the case an' it would be much better for everyone if Fats just takes a coupla inches off his waist. So it is that Fats goes on a very strict diet, which he is very good at doin' as he has much practice at it. He is very good at it except he has this strange idea that the diet only counts for food ya eat ... or, more important, food ya don't eat, locally. Whatever ya eat away from home or the neighborhood does not count for anything. It is a great, big nought. How he comes by such a philosophy I do not know. Maybe he thinks there is someone watchin' what he does from way up there, sort of like a Great Calorie Counter in the sky an' this someone either does not have territorial rights to tally calories outside of yer home turf or maybe he just does not have good peripheral vision. So Fats plays by the rules, an' why not, bein' that they are his own rules, an' eats almost nothin' in Coney Island – from down in the Club we hear his mother wailin', "Mangia! Mangia! Soon you waste away an' become a clothese-a-pin!" – but every night he takes three buses to go to a diner in Canarsie, which is about as far away from Coney Island as Fats'll dare to go. Here, under the watchful eye of no one he consumes huge amounts of food that does not count against his diet an' is only surprised that he is unable to pull his belt even a smidgen tighter, but patience bein' one of Fats' redeemin' virtues, he is willin' to wait.

Fats is a total stranger to Canarsie which is like the eastern outpost of Brooklyn an' a land very different than Coney Island even though both places are known for their rides. In Coney Island, ya take a ride for which you pay a nickel or a dime because it is very excitin' an' you are expectin' to have a real good time an' ya do much yelling an' whoopin' it up. Canarsie is a place where you are taken for a ride for which you do not have to pay anything. It is also excitin' – in a very different way – an' the one thing ya do not expect to have is a good time. There may be much yelling but there is absolutely no whoopin' it up. It is also a place known for its many cemetaries an' many graves with no headstones. Takin' all of this into account, Fats feels that Canarsie is a very safe place for him to eat without it affectin' his diet – not too many eyes will be followin' him here. He also makes very sure to find a diner that sits right next to a bus stop. Even though he knows how healthy walkin' can be, he feels, in this case, it is much healthier not to walk. Canarsie is also a very good place to slink, so ya can imagine

Fats' surprise when on this night he walks inta the diner an' bumps inta
Fivel Finnegan, who lately is doin' a great deal of slinkin'. Neither one
is exactly overjoyed at seein' the other. Not that they have anything
against each other. But to Fivel, it makes him think maybe he is not
slinkin' too well an' Fats is afraid that anything that brings 'home' a
little closer could ruin his diet, which would be terrible after all the
hard work an' effort he puts into it.

Not knowing what else to do, they sit down next to each other at the
counter and it is here that Fivel explains to Fats that he is not exactly
thrilled at the position the Dwarf puts him in.

"I do not wish the guys to think I am a no-action number who is only
mouth 'n hot air. The truth is I am a warm and sensitive human being
who is cut out for administrative or supervisory work – not heavy duty
jobs like paintin' over Louie the Louse."

He assures Fats that if he should perform such a deed, which would
not be any more difficult than scratchin' his nose, people will have a
picture of him that is not in keeping with the true Fivel. "After all, there
is more than one way to skin a cat!"

Fats, whom it does not take too much to impress, is now impressed
as he tries to imagine a skinless Louie the Louse hung up on a clothes
line to dry out.

"Wow! Ain't that somethin'! Here everybody thought you wuz
scared to death an' the truth is, you are a very classy guy who is also
warm an' sensitive – which no one would ever believe about you. In
fact, what could be classier than a guy willin' to walk away from ten G's
rather than besmirch his good name?" This is obviously a real eyebrow-
raiser to Fivel who would not walk away from ten G's if it had a million
volts of electricity runnin' through it. It is just that he knows he cannot
do what the Dwarf sets up for him to do, but that does not mean he does
not wanna get paid for it!

If Fivel Finnegan came with a built-in panic button it would, at this
point, be pressed very hard. "Do not misinterpret what I am implying.
It is just not an act I wish to perform under a spotlight with everyone
looking on. It must be administered very carefully, away from prying

eyes. It is doing something bad in a good way. That's what being an administrator is all about."

Fats goes on, "It is like my momma tells me when we had Spot, our dog – 'Junior', she says ... momma could never understand why everybody calls me Fats ... 'all-a the bad things, you keep away from-a home. Home is only for-a good things.' So, whenever Spot hadda do his poop, we would send him to our neighbor Leo the Dry Cleaner's backyard. An' momma sure wuz right. You shoulda heard our neighbor Leo yowl every time he'd go in his yard an' step in that stuff. Us? We never had that problem. I never forget momma's lesson, Fivel. Bad things ya keep away from home. F'r instance, a diet is a good thing – at least for me it is – so I keep my diet at home, where good things belong. Eatin' is a bad thing when you are on a diet, so I do my eating away from home where it does not affect me. Ya see how it works, Fivel? "

"I think so," Fivel answers, not really havin' the foggiest idea what Fats was talkin' about but makin' a very strong effort to be sociable. "But do ya think it is such a good idea mixin' Spots' poop with yer diet? I know it is only conversation, but even so ...   also, ya said 'when ya had a dog'. I don't ever see ya walkin' no dog. What ever happened to Spot?"

"Oh, Spot? Poor ol' Spot. He ain't no more. My neighbor, Leo the Dry Cleaner, poisoned him. Leo really ain't a Dry Cleaner. The boys just call him that because they say he is a Spot remover."

It is after their third helping of rice pudding, of which all but one has been consumed by Fats, that Fivel remarks, "I am aware that somewhere, mixed in with everything that you have been sayin', there is a point, which, unfortunately, I have not yet gotten."

"As far as you are concerned, Fivel, if doin' in Louie the Louse is such a bad thing because people will think of you in the wrong way, then just do it far away from home. Like ya said – no prying eyes. Remember my momma's lesson – bad things you keep away from home. That way nobody knows or sees exactly what ya done or how ya did it. As far as anyone knows, ya administered him right outta existence, which is good because, like ya said, you are cut out for administerin' or supervisin'.

All the Dwarf wants is ya bring him Louie's vest – he don't care whether ya administered or did a rat-tat-tat. The Dwarf gets the vest – that is good – you get the ten G's – that is good – an' nobody sees how ya really erase Louie the Louse as it is a job you administer far away from home. And because nobody sees it all they know is that you administered the job an' you are still a warm an' sensitive human bein'. Capish?"

Fivel now is, besides bein' a very nervous person, a very exasperated person. "Fats," he explains with more patience than Fivel is generally given credit to have, "I do not think you are gettin' the very best grasp of my predicament. It is much more complex than what you are makin' of it. This actual doin' of the job, sending Louie the Louse on his way – you cannot just call it administerin' an' leave it at that – that is the part that gives me a sour stomach ... "

"I beg your pardon!" Fats, whose height does not exceed his girth by very much, puts a lotta emphasis on what he says by extendin' himself way upward standin' on his tiptoes. "Whattya mean 'you cannot just call it administerin'? You are obviously a person who does not have confidence in his ability when you say you cannot send Louie the Louse on his way by administerin'. I do not know all the technicalities involved – after all, I am not the expert – you are – but I am always readin' in the News or Mirror about how this administration knocks off that administration with – I think it's some kind of car - somethin' called a *coup de tad* or how Father so-an-so administers the Last Rites so some guy can make his journey to heaven in peace ... "

"Where Louie winds up is a much warmer place," Fivel cuts in.

Fats stops as he suddenly makes a realization. "That is it, ain't it? There is no way that Louie the Louse goes to heaven! That is what worries you about administerin', ain't it, Fivel?"

Fivel is so dizzy right now, it is like someone has been spinnin' the counter stool he is sittin' on all night long. Lucky for him, he does not have to answer because Fats is askin' all the questions an' Fats is doin' all the answerin'. "Louie the Louse does not go to heaven," Fats agrees. "That is no problem. It is really all very clear an' simple, Fivel. First, ya gotta get Louie the Louse far from home to do yer administerin' because you do not do any bad or heavy duty stuff near home, and when you are finished, Louie is no longer part of the local scenery as you have dispatched him to a very warm place, which, like you said yourself without no coaching, is what happens to people who do not make it to heaven, an' no one should feel sorry for him because he deserves it. Admit it, Fivel, ain't I a real big help?"

Fats does not get a chance to say another word because just as he finishes pattin' himself on the back Fivel lights up like a street lamp that someone just turns on, grabs Fats by both his ears, pulls his head forward and plants a kiss smack on his lips. Soon as Fats said what he did, little bells started ringin' inside of Fivel's head an' he was ready to start countin' his ten G's. Meanwhile, Fats, who never got kissed on the mouth before, is in a state of shock. With much energy, he is scrubbin' his lips with the back of his hand. "If that is the Kiss of Death – or even a reasonable facsimile – please save it for Louie." "It is because you have showed me the way, Fats! Far away in a very warm place! Did you know you wuz a genius, Fats?"

It is a question that does require some thought. "There were times I suspected it," Fats admitted. "Like a lotta times when I go to the movies on Saturday afternoon an' they have the Dick Tracy chapters. I usually figure out all by myself that the way it ends ain't really the way it ends because if it did, Dick Tracy would never be back next Saturday."

"But this time, Fats," Fivel was beaming, "you outdid yourself. Now five'll getcha ten I can really administer.

CHAPTER TWELVE

THE SLINKER MEETS THE LURKER

Fivel was very excited at that moment, that is true; but as soon as his head finds out what the rest of him is up to, his head takes charge an' will not permit his feet to take him anywhere – especially anywhwere that Louie the Louse might be at. That does not mean that Fivel had a happy head, because Fivel's head wanted the ten G's very badly just like the rest of Fivel, but as it was also in charge of inhalin' an' exhalin' it wanted to make sure that these functions were no way interrupted which one certainly could not bank on if Louie gets wind of Fivel's mission. What Louie does get wind of is that the Dwarf has got him up to his nostrils, a very high place to be, but not exalted, an' has decided that Louie should no longer be part of the community. Even though Louie goes along like the Dwarf doesn't bother him at all, he is not so dumb or brave that he doesn't realize once the Boss gets mad the best place to be is a place very far away from him. This idea is further reinforced when word gets back to Louie that Gertie Gutenyu spills the beans an' he realizes that he is now just another orphan. So, Louie decides to lay low an' see if maybe the Dwarf cools down at all, which, believe me, he does not.

We are just finishin' our Labor Day bash, which, to us is not a very big bash at all as we are not exactly laborers when the Dwarf asks who has seen Fivel. It is three months now since Fivel drew the 'X' an' as far as we all knew there has been no significant change in our population yet. This is when Fats gives us the update about his Canarsie meetin' with Fivel Finnegan. "What're you 'n Fivel doin' meetin' in Canarsie?" Big Nose Sallie wants to know. Fats does not wish to go through the whole explanation about his diet so he thinks very quickly, on a relative basis, of course, an' answers, "Well, Fivel needed someone to help him figure how he will administer Louie the Louse outta existence."

Big Nose Sallie goes all goo-goo eyes, "So he calls on you?" All of us make the sign of the Cross at the same time, sorta like a reflex act – ya know, it was just the natural thing to do. Sallie does not wait for an answer, "If that weasel turns the corner an' runs inta his own shadow he would be scared right outta his shoes 'n sox."

"No! No!" Fats bounces up, wavin' his hands in Big Nose Sallie's face. "Ya got Fivel all wrong. He is a guy with much more class than you would believe." It must be that Fats is rememberin' the kiss on the mouth . "I give him certain ideas, of course, which he gets very excited over an' then he decides how he is gonna administer. You should know, he is very good at supervisin' an' administerin'."

Hearin' this, the Dwarf now comes over, suddenly very interested in this conversation. "Somehow, this does not sound at all like the Fivel we are familiar with. Usually, I think of you as a good boy, Fats, so answer one question for me, please." It is fair to say that Fats, lookin' all the way up at the Dwarf, was not too comfortable at this moment. "Are you on one of your diets now?"

"Wh - why d'ya ask? That is a very personal question, Boss," poor Fats is stammerin' now.

"It is just that when you are on a diet you can get very light-headed from not eating and that would explain what sounds to me like an hallucination."

Fats' eyebrows crinkle an' he thinks for a minute. "Oh, no, Boss. It had nothin' to do with no foreign country. Nothin' like that. It all happened in Canarsie, just like I said." Like I always say, with the Dwarf there is no way of knowin' what he is thinkin' an' this is one time I believe that is very good, especially for Fats. But the Dwarf is not a quitter, so he goes on, "When can I expect him to do this job, Fats? It is goin' on three months now."

"Oh, it should be real soon, Boss. He wuz just figurin' out the very best way of administerin' him from the ideas I gave him," Fats was beamin' with pride. "You should only know he is gonna perform his job with much sensitivity an' warmth." Joey the Clown starts snickerin' at that, "What's Fivel gonna do? Kiss him to death?" Which remark seems to perturb Fats, who for some reason starts turnin' red like a fire engine an' answers in a very defensive way, "Aw, whattya talkin' about? Fivel ain't that kinda guy. He gets very excited over an idea I give him an' tells me he is now ready to administer the job."

"The question is mainly 'when'. We all are aware that some day Louie the Louse can die of old age", Big Nose Sallie asks, with more'n just a little bit of sarcasm.

"Oh, there will be no question marks," Fats assures us. "The deed will be done an' it is Fivel's intention to deposit the vest of Louie the Louse right inta the Boss' hands like he promised. It will be proof positive. Ya gotta unnerstand, Fivel is a much classier an' much more honorable gent than we give him credit for."

At this Big Nose Sallie's eyebrow gets a little arch to it an' he nods his head, sorta like he is sayin', "Aha! Now I see." Salvatore Pignasale does somethin' most of the other guys do not do at all – he thinks. What he is thinkin' at this exact moment I am not sure of. Not only am I not sure of it – I do not even have an inkling. But there is absolutely no question in my mind that the wheels inside of Sallie's head are turnin'. With the Dwarf, ya never know what is goin' on inside his head because his face tells no tales. Big Nose Sallie, on the other hand, although not prone to giggles or cryin' jags, is a guy who once in a while does show a sign of emotion here 'n there. By now I know that when Sallie's eyebrow goes inta that half-moon stretch an' he gives with a little twisted smile he is feelin' the way I do when I look at my hand and see a full house. It is a feelin' of 'I gotcha'. Sallie's 'I gotcha' is usually like his mind is dealt a full house – ya know, it suddenly puts everything

together an' Sallie can start haulin' in his pot. Like I said, I have no idea
what Sallie is thinkin' about an' maybe even Sallie himself hasn't got
it a hundred per cent put together yet but that look is there an' ya know
sooner or later he is gonna be playin' his hand – whatever it is.

Right now, Fivel Finnegan wants to play his hand, too. It is a big
pot, ten G's, an' he is holdin' good cards which he didn't even realize
until his talk with Fats Suozzo. But what he wants to do an' what he
can do are not at all related to each other. It is like maybe he should be
in an Iron Lung because he is totally paralyzed just thinkin' about what
he has to do. He knows there is a reason for this paralysis. It is not
too difficult for him to figure it out. In fact it is simple – he is scared
to death. He is not so much afraid of meetin' with an accident. It is a
well-planned execution that worries him ... an' all the pain an' torture
that probably goes along with it. These are things that Louie the Louse
is reputed to be very good at an' even if Fivel wanted to question the
accuracy of such a reputation he would be much more comfortable not
doin' it as the subject.

Fats reminds Fivel that once Louie the Louse is removed from the
scene an' the Dwarf is presented with his red plaid vest as proof, the
ten G's are due an' payable. Then when Fats adds the part about dis-
patchin' him to a very warm place everything suddenly adds up for
Fivel. For Fats, 'a real warm place' is the natural alternative when
he realizes there will be no openings in heaven for Louie the Louse.
Fivel has no problem with the thought of Louie burnin' in Hell; he
only has a problem with the thought of him bein' the one to send him
there. If anything goes wrong between the thinkin' of it an' the doin'
of it – that is what causes Fivel's paralysis – just thinkin' of what happens if somethin' does go wrong... It is understandable to Fivel, that if
he approaches Louie the Louse an' says, "I am sendin' you on yer way
to Hell" that Louie the Louse could possibly take offense an' respond
in a way most unkind. But, on the other hand, if Fivel were to extend
an invitation to another warm place – just let us say as a for instance,
Miami Beach – it may bring forth a somewhat different response. Not
in the wildest stretchin' of his imagination could Fivel picture someone

wantin' to kill ya for askin' if ya would like to go to Miami Beach. I would not necessarily consider this to be an absolute, but why upset Fivel? So, Fivel, who is definitely a creature of survival, from the minute Fats gives him the idea, works out in his head this plan which he knows is fool-proof, an idea for which any day in the week, five'll get-cha ten it works. Now, as it is important for Fivel to convince himself of the wisdom of carryin' out his plan, he calls a meeting of all the parts of himself, to which he gets a full turnout as he was most confident he would. His mouth is very brave but when it comes to his brain, his guts an' his backbone, there is much opposition. It is only when he points out to himself that the choices are to carry out his plan with Louie the Louse or to face the wrath of the Dwarf if he doesn't that he winds up gettin' a unanimous but reluctant go for it.

Louie the Louse, although not strictly a creature of survival, doesn't exactly pooh-pooh it. He is a combination of alley-cat, rat an' rattle snake whose good qualities you do not need a pen or pencil an' paper to list, or a good memory to remember them with because if you just list one you are talkin' about somebody else. But even if it is nothin' but instinct, he wants to be around to do some hurtin' another day. It is not that he is sorry for the things he does – it is the only way he knows to be. All he is sorry about is that the Dwarf is finally on his case an' how much healthier it would be if there was a lot of distance between them. It is for this reason that Louie follows a pattern that is not too very different from the pattern followed by Fivel Finnegan. While Fivel has become a slinker, Louie the Louse is now a lurker an' at times even a prowler. A slinker hides in shadows only to survive, but a lurker can use the same shadows to survive with much more sinister intentions. So the two of them go hoppin' their way, shadow to shadow, neither seekin' fame or glory at this moment. As there are only so many shadows around, it is only natural that many shadows are used for both slinkin' an' lurkin' an' also there are overlappin' shadows so it is no great wonder that occas-sionally a slinker an' a lurker come together in overlappin' or concentric shadows.

****

It was a dark an' moonless night with the fog rollin' in from the ocean when two shadow-dwellers happen upon each other on one of Coney Island's most shadowy streets, Bowery Street, which sits between Surf Avenue an' the Boardwalk. Truthfully, I am not at all certain of the weather conditions on this particular evenin' but these are the conditions that are usually around in such situations. Durin' the spring an' summer season Bowery Street is the brightest, liveliest place in all of New York. It is a combination circus midway, amusement park an' cabaret. But not too long after Labor Day all the neon lights are turned off, shutters are pulled down an' it is a perfect place to go if you are lookin' to have yer hair parted by a whiskey bottle, probably not Chivas Regal. It is also not too bad a place to go if ya do not wish to be noticed by the Dwarf, who gives to the people he knows credit for more smarts than to take a stroll down Bowery Street. So it is that out of the shadows, out of the fog inta who knows what kind of adventures step Fivel Finnegan an' Louie the Louse.

If anyone invents a Fright-Meter an' tries it out at this encounter, for sure this instrument will never be used again because its top will be blown completely away from measuring a yowl that comes outta Fivel which, on Fifty-Second Street's Jazz Row, to where I am certain this scream carried, it maybe was thought to be some wild vocalist tryin' to keep up with a New Orleans jam session but in Coney Island, a place where shouts from the Cyclone, the Wonder Wheel an' the Parachute Jump make shouts of any kind to be ignored as normal, everyday occurrences, ambulances were wailin' an' runnin' back an' forth all night due to a sudden an' unexplained outbreak of heart failure. Louie the Louse does not exactly take this nocturnal meeting in stride, either. He is not a yowler but he gives a jump so high that if anyone has the chance to measure it, he probably breaks the world and Olympic pole vault record without a pole.

When the hair on top of Fivel's head stops standin' at attention an' the blood in his veins thaws out an' starts flowin' again, he somehow gets his mouth, which is always the most active part of him, to work. "Louie, what a pleasant surprise bumpin' inta you like this."

"Ya didn't bump inta nobody. Got it, runt?" It was surprisin' how much more civil an' polite Louie was than usual. "If I hear that anyone finds out ya seen me, people will be sayin' - 'Remember that guy named Fivel? Wonder whatever happened to him.' "

It is not too difficult to put a scare inta Fivel but he is a coward with qualifications. He is more afraid of losin' out on the ten G's than he is of Louie the Louse. He knows that this is his big chance an' he gotta play his cards right. What Louie just says to him does not make him feel very good, that is true, so to make himself feel a little better he tries to think of happy things – like his last birthday. This only makes him more depressed when he thinks if he does not play his cards right, it very probably could be his last birthday.

"That was very funny, Louie," Fivel comes back with a bigger bluff than he ever uses at a poker table, "but I cannot stand aroun' an' exchange jokes with ya all night."

Louie gives this big blink an' does a double take, "If ya hear what I said as a joke, wait 'til ya get the punch line – it'll probably kill ya."

Fivel thinks to himself, "It is terrible what a guy gotta put up with just to make ten G's," after which he says to Louie, "Well, it's really been nice bumpin' inta ya like this but I really gotta go now as I am preparin' to take leave of this town for much greener pastures." For a second he thinks someone must be doin' a flamenco dance as he is hearin' castanets from very nearby – then he realizes it is only the sound of his knees knockin'.

"Hold yer horses, Fivel," Louie barks. "This meetin' ain't over till I dismiss everybody. What is this 'leavin' town for greener pastures garbage'?" There is suddenly a sign of much interest in Louie's voice.

"Please, let us not dwell on what I have just said as it is sort of a secret, Louie. It is somethin' I am not lookin' to spread aroun'." Fivel is now like the fisherman danglin' the bait an' it is one big hungry fish ready to bite at it.

"What kinda secrets can there be between best friends, Fivel?" It is obvious to Fivel that some of Gertie Gutenyu's actin' ability hadda rub off on Louie, who continues, "It is a very strong coincidence that I, too, am lookin' to pack in New York for a while."

"Reasons of health?" Fivel asks with much innocence.

Louie thinks for a minute before he answers, conjurin' up this picture of the Dwarf's ham-hock of a hand closin' in on him, then he nods his head, "I guess ya could call it that. Nothin' serious, ya unnerstan'."

"Oh, it is better ya don't ignore," Fivel warns. "Ya never know what can become life-threatenin'. That is why it is so important to live in a really good climate, especially if ya can also rake in the jack at the same time. I feel most fortunate to be in just such a position now. Whoops! Me 'n my big mouth. I didn't learn my lesson when I blab this to the Dwarf. My mouth is always flappin' in the wind." Fivel is very proud of himself at this moment as he had no Gertie Gutenyu whose actin' ability could rub off on him but it is two months of practicin' these lines in front of a mirror that now pays off.

"The Dwarf?" The hungry fish is not just gobblin' up the bait now. He is takin' the whole hook, line an' sinker. "What is this story about greener pastures an' rakin' in the jack that you have blabbed to the Dwarf?"

"Nah! I told ya – it is a secret."

"Fivel, like I said, friends have no secrets."

"It is enough I got the Dwarf pleadin' to be let in on it an' he makes me promise not to talk about it to anyone else," Fivel keeps settin' the table for Louie. "He says it is like havin' the key to Fort Knox. You would not respect me if I betray his trust."

Louie the Louse is now champin' at the bit. "I would, Fivel. I would. I would respect ya a lot. On the other hand, as a desperate person with health problems that are presently not serious but as you pointed out, can become life-threatenin', you may force me to choke the secret out of you, which I do not wish to do but it may be necessary for my survival."

Thinkin' of Knuckles McTavish an' Honest Otto the Pawnbroker, Fivel feels he should not test Louie the Louse too far. "Not wishin' to aggravate a sick friend, I will divulge my secret, but only to let it serve as an inspiration to you – I am going to Miami Beach."

Louie's face drops almost to the floor. "What happened to Fort Knox?"

"Fort Knox was only an anthology, Louie," Fivel explains with much patience, "as ya can scoop up gold just as easy in Miami as if ya was locked in Fort Knox."

"Ya don't say!" Louie is bug-eyed now. "How is that?"

" When ya got a town that has as many tracks an' other gamblin' establishments, like the dogs, jai-alai an' where even Bingo is big-time ya better get a king-size bed because ya gonna need a lotta mattress to stuff."

"So, what exactly is the nature of your trip there?" Louie asks, tryin' very hard to hide his enthusiasm.

Fivel grins and lowers his eyes so his humility will not be lost on Louie. "I have decided to open up Miami as a new base of operations an' the Dwarf is pleadin' that I take him in as a partner. It will make New York a spit in the bucket. Ya got shop owners who got nobody to offer them protection an a million ol' people, I mean people in their seventies an' eighties, an army of octopusses, with their pension checks burnin' a hole in their pockets an' there is nobody even doin' a good numbers business there. These poor people get no service at all. It will be like pickin' over-ripe fruit from the tree. Very over-ripe fruit – it is like a city of ol' geezers jus' waitin' to be taken. It only presents two problems for me."

"Yeah? What kinda problems can ya have with such a situation?"

"Well, it is probably unique with me, ya know, like my own personality traits." Fivel is so wrapped up in the story he is weavin' now that he is actually believin' what he is spoutin'. "First, there is not enough of a challenge involved here for me. It is all gonna be so easy. An' then there is the question of how a softie such as myself is gonna handle the easy pickin's that I take from the social security set. A conscience is a terrible thing to have to live with."

It is at this point that Louie the Louse's eyes light up. "Boy! I would have no such problems. Bein' a person in need of rest an' relaxation I do not need challenges in my life at this time. An' I absolutely agree with ya that a conscience is a terrible thing to have to live with – so I do not. Maybe ya should be thinkin' about me as a partner, Fivel." He is already thinkin' how easy it would be gettin' rid of the little weasel once they get to Miami.

"Well, I don't know, Louie ..." Fivel cups his chin in his hand, like he is in deep thought considerin' what Louie the Louse proposes, also thinkin' what he knows Louie is thinkin' about if an' when they get to Miami. "I did not give the Dwarf an answer because I do not like the arrangement. I will be down there doin' everything, which is not too bad to swallow, because it is like the Garden of Eden, but why do I need a partner who will never come down there an' will share in everything. Ya know, the Dwarf hates hot weather. They say he cannot function in it an' there is absolutely nothin' that can get him down there. Also, I have so many things goin' for me up here that I cannot jus' pick up an' go. An' if I do not take the Dwarf in on this an' I take you in instead, I am only sayin' 'if'", Fivel emphasizes, " I do not think the Dwarf would be very crazy about such an idea. He is not exactly fond of you, ya know."

Now Louie is just about salivatin', he is so hungry to horn in. "He does not have to know, Fivel." He is already thinkin' to himself how it would feel to put this one over on the big stoop. "Like ya said, whaddya need a partner who will do nothin' but share yer profits. Now, with me as a partner ya can attend to whatever ya have to up here an' I will take care of everything in Miami once ya teach me what has to be done an' tell me where everythin' is at."

"I don't know, Louie. If the Dwarf gets wind of this ... "

"There is nothin' to get wind of," Louie the Louse cuts in with somethin' between a plea an' a threat. "I will stay tucked away in Miami quiet like a mouse." It is obvious that Louie has no intention of takin' 'no' for an answer. Only to Fivel is it obvious that he has no intention of givin' 'no' for an answer.

An' so it is that this pie-in-the-sky partnership is cemented with two franks with the works an' two root beers at Nathan's, for which the tab is picked up by Fivel as Louie the Louse has this physical condition that does not permit his hands to come within two feet of his pockets. Fivel then makes all the necessary arrangements which inlude a train ticket, one way, of course, an' a phone call to his sister Flossie, collect, of course, in Miami Beach, to let her know she will be havin' a house guest for an indeterminate stay. Actually, Fivel does not know for how long he can keep the wool pulled over Louie's eyes but he does not care once he collects the ten G's. Flossie is not too thrilled at this arrangement as havin' grown up in Coney Island she had certain memories of Louie the Louse, none of which can be described as fond. Who could ever forget this kid who, every afternoon, would drag this horrible-smellin' dog on a leash an' walk back an' forth so ya'd almost puke from the stink until, finally ya'd pay him to walk somewhere else. An' there was no point in tellin' him to bathe the dog, because no amount of bathin' an' perfume is gonna help once a dog is dead for almost two years. There were just too many strange things about this Louie but she could never say 'no' to her brother because ya could never be sure when he would keep his word an' hold his breath till he died.

It is now time to get the show on the road, Fivel realizes. "Ya may as well give up yer apartment now, Louie. No sense payin' rent for somethin' yer not gonna be needin' anymore."

Louie looks up in surprise. "Rent? Who pays rent?"

"Whaddya mean 'Who pays rent?' " Now it is Fivel's turn to be surprised. "Don't yer landlord come aroun' an' ask ya for the rent at the beginnin' of every month?"

"He useta," Louie does not quite look Fivel in the eye right now, "then he became an absentee landlord an' does not come aroun' anymore."

"How does a guy become an absentee landlord an' let ya live there without payin' rent?" Fivel is really curious now. Louie the Louse just shrugs but does not answer an' again Fivel finds himself thinkin' about Knuckles McTavish an' Honest Otto an' thinks maybe he should change the subject a little bit. "There is not much to pack when ya live in Miami," Fivel says, "as it is a very, very warm place."

"That's good," Louie says, really waitin' for Fivel to spring for another frank, of which there is very little chance of happenin', "I like travelin' light – I think, as I have never traveled before."

Fivel knows this gotta come out right, as everything else was just workin' up to it. He runs his fingers along the lapel edges of Louie's red plaid vest an' hopes there is not a catch in his voice as he says, "This feels like really good material. It must be pretty warm, huh, Louie?"

Louie looks down at his pride 'n joy vest. "Oh, yeah, it is very good material – an' very warm. It is made in Scotland, ya know," he beams.

At this moment Fivel feels like a matador raisin' his blade for the final thrust. "It would certainly be outta place in Miami as such a fashionplate as yerself must know, as it will cause ya to sweat to death. I know I would not want big, salty perspiration stains on such a fine vest."

Louie the Louse seems now to be genuinely concerned. "No, I do not want anything to happen to this vest."

Fivel gives with this great, expansive smile, holds out his hand an' says, "Gimme the vest for safe keepin', an' any other clothes ya cannot use there. I will keep it in perfect shape for ya."

Louie's expression starts as one of doubt but soon it changes to what best can be described as horror as he clutches his hands protectively around his vest. "Oh, no! I couldn't do that, Fivel. I go nowhere without my vest. It is like part of my skin! Things will work itself out."

Fivel, on the other hand, has to hide his feelin' of horror. But no way is Louie the Louse gonna get another Nathan's frank!

JOEY THE CLOWN LEARNS PROTOCOL

In my mind, there is no two ways about it. We gotta call in the linoleum man right away for an estimate as Big Nose Sallie has worn out the whole middle of our floor by walkin' back 'n forth from mornin' to night. It is obvious he is in very deep thought ever since Fats reports on his meetin' with Fivel Finnegan an' assures us that Fivel will come through an' when Big Nose Sallie is thinkin' he lubricates his brain by walkin' . This method of thinkin' is nowhere as enjoyable as mine, which requires the devourin' of huge amounts of food but I must agree that it is less fattenin'. Actually, there is much more scientific logic backin' my method as the jaw an' the mouth use muscles in the head that are also probably connected to the brain, an' therefore exercise the brain, whereas walkin' uses muscles much lower down that are nowhere near the brain. Anyhow, I do not look to make light of Sallie's methods an' I am certainly not lookin' to diminish his ability as a wise person. The fact remains, Sallie is greatly bothered as things just do not seem to add up to him concernin' Fivel an' the task he is to perform.

It is not that he has any answers. He does not. But he does know Fivel well enough to be sure that he can have no enthusiasm for the job at hand even with the reward. He also knows Fivel well enough to figure that he will weasel an' squirm his way aroun' an' do everything in his power, no matter how unthinkable, to get his grubby hands on the ten G's without doin' the job. With these thoughts rollin' aroun' in his head, Big Nose Sallie knows he cannot just keep walkin' back 'n forth but he gotta do somethin' to find out what Fivel is really up to, so he makes his move an' decides to enlist the services of the Clown. My immediate thought is maybe he is better off to keep walkin' back 'n forth.

Lately, I observe, the Clown is not a very happy person. He spends much of his time sittin' on a stool at the counter, munchin' on peanuts an' he, too, seems to be in very deep thought which is an occupation not usually indulged in by him so when Big Nose Sallie converses with him the Clown is so involved in his thinkin' that he does not hear a word. Finally, Big Nose Sallie gives him a major clunk on the cranium with a rolled-up newspaper to which the Clown responds first, with a jump on his stool, then, rubbin' the top of his wounded head, gripes, "Hey, whatja whack me for, Salvatore?"

"You know, I am talkin' to you for five minutes," Sallie exaggerates, "an' it is like talkin' to a corpse. I am just makin' sure that you are alive, a fact I am still not a hundred per cent certain of."

"Ya should know, Sallie," the Clown assures him," that I am, at this moment, alive, but another bop or two like that," he continues rubbin' his head, "an' that situation very easily changes."

"I am sorry," Sallie apologizes, "but I was really under the assumption that was the safest place to hit ya. Anyhow, I really wanna talk to you about something I would like ya to do. I figure you are the only one I can depend upon."

Such flattery makes no impression on the Clown. "I am sorry, Salvatore. I cannot do anything for anyone right now as I am a very depressed an' troubled person."

If Big Nose Sallie is not genuinely touched, he does not let on. "I am very sorry to hear such news, Joey. I find it to be most distressing that a friend such as you is not happy and fully content with his life. Do you wish to confide in me an' explain what it is that is troublin' you so?"

"Actually, maybe ya can help," the Clown perks up a little. "You got real smarts, Sallie. Maybe you can tell me what I should do."

Sallie shrugs an' waits an' the Clown goes on, "Ya see, it is a matter of protocol."

"A matter of protocol?" It is obvious that Big Nose Sallie is somewhat impressed. Whether he is impressed at the fact that Joey the Clown could be troubled over such a thing or whether he is impressed at Joey's command of our mother tongue I do not know but his look is one of much more respect than I would expect he shows to the Clown. "What is this matter of protocol we are talkin' about, Joey?"

Joey is not overly anxious to continue this conversation. He hangs his head, waits a minute but finally answers, "Aw, you know about my impendin' marriage to Goldie ..."

"I have heard mention of it," Sallie acknowledges, "from the mouth of Goldie when we were visitin' you at the hospital. I cannot say that I, as well as everybody else, was not greatly surprised – especially takin' into account that we know you to be an already married man. Has there possibly been a change in your family makeup, Joey?"

"Oh, no," Joey answers very quickly, with no hesitation. "My ol' lady, Angie, she don't wear no makeup at all except to cover a zit here 'n there."

Big Nose Sallie is no longer impressed like he was just a minute ago. "Well, I guess that answers my question in a sorta roundabout way. Angie is still your wife, right?"

"Naturally. If there wuz a wake don't ya think you woulda been invited?"

Big Nose Sallie is experiencin' somethin' he goes through very often when talkin' to the Clown – he is becomin' very exasperated. "Joey, you just cannot be married to two women – it is a sin!"

The Clown pushes that aside with a wave of his hand. "Ah, that won't hardly count. I got so many bad marks chalked up already, havin' two wives won't mean a thing."

"If that doesn't bother you," Sallie wantsa know, "then what does? What is it with this protocol?"

"I am very bothered ," the Clown begins to explain, "because I do not know the proper way of handlin' this situation as it is a long time between weddin's for me. It involves the guest list – I do not know if I should invite Angie or not. It is not that I think she will have a good time an' she probably will not even bring a gift but I do not wish to hurt nobody's feelin's by not doin' the right thing." This conversation has now become so intriguin' to us that we just put our cards down on the table, leave our money sittin' there and walk over by Sallie to get a better earful of the Clown's dilemma. Sallie, meanwhile, looks like he is almost punchdrunk an' in need of smellin' salts but somehow manages to ask, "Ya mean to tell me that your wife Angie knows you are gettin' married?"

"Oh, I don't think so, Sallie. We are a very quiet sorta family what doesn't discuss much except like 'What's for dinner?' an' the fact that I am a bum – that is her distorted opinion, of course ..." Joey waits for a minute to let this sink in, then he goes on, "In fact, she thinks alla my friends are bums, even a classy guy like you, Sallie!"

About some things, Sallie can be a very vain person so it seems this does offend him a bit. "Me, a bum! Why would she say such a thing?"

"Don't take it to heart," the Clown tries to comfort him. "Ever since Oldsmobile comes out with that new transmission – ya know, no clutch an' no first, second or third gears – whenever she wantsa mouth off to me about somethin', which is almost always, she starts hollerin' about me an' my Hydramatic friends ..."

We are all somewhat puzzled now but Sallie asks, "What does that mean, Hydramatic friends?"

"Forget it," the Clown shrugs. "That is her way of callin' ya a bunch of shiftless bums."

Sallie, pointin' his finger at Joey, says, "I think you are tryin' to turn us against Angie by talkin' this way. But it will not work. The institution of marriage is sacred an' cannot be taken lightly."

"Hey," the Clown is now on the defensive, "whattya makin' me the bad guy for? Don't everyone here have a doll on the side?"

"Yeah," Sallie responds, "but we don't marry them. We only got one wife. Havin' a doll on the side gives your wife a chance to rest an' take proper care of the family. It is neither good nor wise to use up your wife. It is just like in a ballgame – ya got a startin' pitcher, when he gets tired, ya don't wanna ruin him – ya bring in a relief pitcher. That is the same reason we got a doll on the side."

"So, ya never heard of makin' a relief pitcher yer startin' pitcher?" The Clown is now lookin' around for approval at this one.

Sallie drapes his arm aroun' the Clown's shoulder which immediately has him talkin' with much more authority. It is a little touch I have seen Big Nose Sallie use many times before. "Ya know, Joey, you an' Angie shoulda had kids. Kids are what make for a strong family. It is never too late."

"Nah," Joey answers, "Angie don't want no kids."

"What do you mean - 'Angie don't want no kids' - every woman wants kids."

"I am tellin' ya," Joey repeats, "Angie don't want no kids. She got this crazy thing about not wantin' kids because she don't want me givin' them my hand-me-down clothes."

This is one very quiet room. Sallie is almost afraid to ask, but he does, anyhow. "Angie doesn't want children because she doesn't want you givin' them your hand-me-down clothes. Joey, I have never heard of such a thing."

"Whattya want from me? I ain't the one who said it. I am just repeatin' it. Angie is the one who said it!"

"An' that is exactly what she said?" Big Nose Sallie is simply not buyin' this one an' either are the rest of us. "Joey, it is very difficult to believe."

"Don't I know that!" Joey is quick to agree on this point. "It is so stupid. My clothes won't even fit no kids."

"I don't mean for that reason," Sallie explains. "I mean it is difficult to believe that is the reason why Angie would not want kids. Tell me, how did she say it, Joey?"

"I told ya! What're we doin', playin' a game? She said – D' you think I would have any kids that you're gonna hand your old clothes down to!"

"Just like that?" Sallie asks. "It was just because of your old clothes. Plain old clothes?"

A glimmer of memory comes back to the Clown. "In fact it wasn't just any clothes. She didn't want me givin' them my dungarees. Ain't that somethin'? When did you ever see me wearin' dungarees?"

Big Nose Sallie smiles, workin' very hard to squeeze this one outta the Clown. "Think, Joey, just think. Exactly how did she say it? Close yer eyes so ya can think better."

"Okay. Okay," the Clown is sayin' softly with his eyes closed an' all of us leanin' forward so we don't miss a word. "That's it. Now I got it exactly. I tell Angie about a year after we are married that my mother thinks it is a good idea that we start raisin' a family an' Angie gives this big laugh an' yells, 'You think I'm crazy enough to have any kids who'll have your genes handed down to them?' I try to tell her that I only wear good slacks from Ripley Brothers but it cuts no ice at all."

Bein' a realist, Sallie sees no reason to pursue this avenue any further. There is no point in tryin' to convince the Clown to raise a family. But to Sallie it is still important to check out his hunch that all is not exactly copasetic with Fivel huntin' down Louie the Louse. An' he is still of the feelin' that the Clown is the best-suited person to act as his blood-hound as there are absolutely no nerve endings throughout the Clown's body ... he does not fear, he does not scare, he does not care. It is for this reason that Sallie negotiates with the Clown an' when it comes to negotiatin', Sallie is strictly a front-runner. There are numerous merchants out there who, they say, can sell ya the Brooklyn Bridge but only Big Nose Sallie would package it with a two-year service contract, paid up front, of course. With the Clown, he tells him - do not worry, put a smile on yer puss an' I will work out yer problem for ya. It is a statement that certainly pumps the Clown up an' he inquires how Sallie can make such a promise, when it is really a double problem as it involves two women – not just one – to which Sallie says not to worry, when Sallie says a problem will be worked out, it will be worked out no matter if a hundred women were involved. All the Clown has to do is get on the tail of Fivel Finnegan an' see what the weasel is really up to.

So it is, on that eventful eve, when two shadows overlapped on Bowery Street there was a third, very large, very solitary, somewhat unnoticable shadow, an' it was in this shadow that the Clown is tucked away while he spends his time followin' behind the shadow in which was slinkin' Fivel Finnegan. When the Clown returns to the Mermaid Social Athletic Club an' Big Nose Sallie inquires as to whether he has seen or heard anything unusual or interestin', Joey informs Sallie, "Unusual? You bet yer life. I follow Fivel an' he bumps smack inta Louie the Louse on the block before the boardwalk." He now has Sallie's full, undivided attention. "An' what is unusual," the Clown continues, "is that ... no, it is more 'n unusual, it is unbelievable ... Fivel Finnegan springs for two Nathan's hot dogs!" Sallie's eyes are buggin' outta his head, which, when the Clown sees, he gives a big grin, "I knew ya wouldn't believe it! That is exactly how I felt, Salvatore." What the Clown does not bring up is how close he is to blowin' his cover in the hopes that he, too, maybe will be treated to a hot dog by Fivel, but realizin' the nature of whom he is dealin' with he stays incognito, although salivatin' heavily. Sallie, who does not give inta anger very often is now ready to explode.

"What is this with a menu rundown? I do not send you out for a report on Fivel's dinin' habits. I want to know what Fivel does when he comes across Louie the Louse. Does he try to take him out?"

"Not right there," the Clown answers. "It looks to me like he is settin' him up to knock him off outta town. An' like Fats said, he is lookin' to make sure he presents his vest inta the Boss' hands. Ya know Fivel, he wantsa make sure he collects that ten G's."

"What makes you think he is lookin' to knock him off outta town?" Big Nose Sallie wantsa know.

"Well," the Clown says, givin' his version of what he hears, "I think he is of the opinion that nobody outta New York knows him or Louie so when they find Louie's body in Fort Knox..."

"Fort Knox?" Sallie forgets when you are dealin' with the Clown you get a very liberal translation of what transpires.

"That is what I said," the Clown assures him. "It is obvious he is playin' on Louie the Louse's greed to get him away from here, probably so he can do his number on him in an outta the way place where, because he is not at all known, he feels nobody connects him to it. It is also obvious he is lookin' to leave no doubt in the Dwarf's mind an' that is why he knows he gotta strip Louie of the vest."

This extreme generosity of the Dwarf's as to acceptin' Louie the Louse's vest in lieu of his head or just a good old fashioned public blow-away is causin' Big Nose Sallie much grief. The picture of exchangin' ten G's for a vest with no corpus delecti does not exactly thrill him to the core. What he hears from the Clown only reinforces his feelin' that the Dwarf has just left the door open wide enough for a weasel to squirm through an' it is up to him, Big Nose Sallie, to close that opening.

Meanwhile, the Clown, though heavy of heart, performs what is asked of him and Big Nose Sallie, always true to his word, keeps his end of the bargain too. If anything, he keeps his end of the bargain too well. He promises the Clown to work out his problem for him an' sure enough, that problem – whether to invite his wife to his wedding – is no longer a problem. This we find out at the same time we find out that the Clown sleeps on Bugs Bunny bedsheets, which is what we find him snoozin' on on the sofa by the pool table just a coupla days after his intelligence work for Big Nose Sallie. Backtrackin' for a moment let us amend that 'intelligence work' to somethin' like 'undercover job' or 'cloak an' dagger mission' as it is the Clown we are speakin' of. When he wakes up, which he does as soon as Fats Suozzo sits down on him, not noticin' the Clown as the lights are not yet turned on, the first thing he says is, "Ouch! Ya know, Fats, you really make quite an impression on a person!" which he soon follows with, "Can you guys please keep it down as this is now my temporary residence."

Now, nobody can say Big Nose Sallie is not one very efficient, effective worker who covers every base an' leaves no stone unturned. Although, this is a situation he would never involve himself in under ordinary circumstances, once he makes the committment, it is not a half-hearted effort as that is not Big Nose Sallie's way. In fact, there is even a certain amount of feelin' involved here, as Sallie does not take lightly things such as loyalty to Mother, country, family an' friends. So, Sallie approaches his task with much fervor an' gusto, leavin' as little as possible to chance by tacklin' both parts of Joey's problem – Goldie an' Angie. He calls first on Angie, like he is lookin' for Joey, who he knows will not be there. Now, ya gotta admit, invitin' yer wife to yer wedding to someone else, which, of course, yer wife knows nothin' about, is not the easiest of things to pull off. It is somethin' that can result in loss of speech, a shock to the system an', of course, death. Sallie figures, in order to prepare Angie for such a bizarre event, he gotta point out to her that Joey is a most bizarre character. In doin' so, he informs Angie that Joey is not deservin' of a wife with all the good qualities that she possesses an' she should achieve sainthood for puttin' up with him all these years. Hopefully, in Sallie's mind, this will soften the blow for Angie. What happens, though, is she is in such total agreement with Big Nose Sallie, it is like her eyes have been opened up for her an' she says to herself, "Yeah, I am too good for that bum!" with which she packs his things includin' his Bugs Bunny bedding, dumps them in the hallway an' changes the locks on the door.

At this point it seems that Big Nose Sallie has done his job an' solved the Clown's problem for him. Only Sallie, as I said, is one very thorough worker who does not yet know the result of his talk with Angie DiCollonna, so he embarks on phase two of his plan to solve the Clown's problem an' takes a cab to Junior's so he can talk to Goldie. With Goldie he goes about it just the opposite of how he does with Angie. That is because in Big Nose Sallie's mind he gotta lean over more on the side of Angie, who is legally attached to Joey, than to Goldie, who after all is interferin' with sacred vows, although he does not really fault Goldie as she does not even know that the Clown is married. When Sallie questions the Clown on this subject by askin' him point blank, "Doesn't Goldie ever ask if you are married?" the Clown responds, "Not exactly. What she says is – 'A guy like you never gets married?' – An' as I do not know any guys like me I answer very honestly, even though I keep my fingers crossed just in case, – 'Nope. I guess not.'" Actually, what Big Nose Sallie does with Goldie is to make her feel guilty in a different sorta way. He explains to her that the Clown is really a free spirit to whom marriage would be like clippin' the wings of a butterfly. His trademarks of loyalty, bravery an' derring-do would all be smothered if his freedom were taken from him. It would be a disservice to everyone he touches upon. He makes it almost like she gotta understand that at this time in her life she is not yet worthy of such a noble creature as the Clown an' if she joins in such a union before she is ready for it, it will only result in much regrets an' misgivings for her. He says all of this to Goldie never removin' his eyes from the strawberry cheesecake which she has set before him on the counter and on which he almost chokes deliverin' such a spiel. He does not wish to drive her to tears, especially when she tells him the cheesecake is on the house, an' Goldie will not be driven to tears.

What Sallie does not know is that as the wedding date draws nearer, Goldie, although she does not walk barefoot in the snow an' shows no signs of frostbite, seems to be gettin' cold feet. It is not that her feelings for Joey the Clown change. It is that here she is, a girl from Hoboken, makin' her own way in the Big City, always doin' whatever she wanted an' never able to take orders from anyone, especially Joey, suddenly faced with havin' to love, honor an' obey. An' she is the one who will be clippin' the wings from a butterfly? So, no tears go rollin' down her cheeks at Big Nose Sallie's lecture. Instead, Sallie can have all the cheesecake in Junior's kitchen at no charge, especially as this will be Goldie's last night there.

LOUIE AND GOLDIE GO SOUTH

Probably, if Big Nose Sallie gets to the Club before the mailman he would be greeted in a completely different manner, but as the mailman gets there first what Sallie finds out is that the Clown is not truly appreciative of all the time an' effort he puts inta solvin' the Clown's problems. He does not even get both feet inside the door before the Clown is bouncin' in front of him, wavin' a letter in his face. "I gotta hand it to ya, Salvatore. Ya sure are one big help. I just gotta remember if I ever get a cold, never to ask you for advice on how to get rid of it – if I do, I'll probably die of pneumonia!"

"This is a Thank You?" Sallie asks in wide-eyed innocence. "I think I would see more appreciation from a guy strapped in the electric chair to the guy throwin' the switch."

"Ya better believe it! He would be sufferin' a lot less pain!" The Clown emphasizes what he says by continuin' to wave the letter in Big Nose Sallie's face. "In two days, with your help, I lose my ol' lady, my apartment, most of my clothes ..." an' still wavin' the letter, "an' now Goldie! My dear friend, Salvatore, you have made me an orphan!"

Sallie shrugs, "This I do not understand. All I said to Goldie was nice things about you, Joey. Let me see that letter."

What Joey hands Sallie is a one-page note addressed to Joseph DiCollonna at the Club as Goldie does not know the Clown's home address. The ink is smudged in a way that would make many people call it a tear-stained letter but it is my personal feeling that you would find no salt on these smudges because drops of water from your kitchen faucet will not leave salt. The Dear Joey letter is as follows - "After talking with your very good friend Salvatore I realized how selfish it was of me to even think of depriving you your freedom. It is important at this time that you be there for everyone as you are truly a free spirit and I cannot live with it on my conscience that I shackled you and kept you from performing your deeds of bravado. Our love, if it is as strong as I believe it to be, will transcend all and in time we will be united. But first I must prove myself to be worthy of your love and companionship. It is imperative that I grow as a person. I must do a great deal of growing to be worthy of one such as you." It is at this point that the Clown interrupts Sallie's reading of the letter with what, I gotta admit, is not an inappropriate question. "What is it with this 'I must do a great deal of growing'? Hey, Salvatore, make sure that letter is addressed to me an' not to the Dwarf. I mean, how much d' ya think she can grow an' still wear high heels with me?"

"Okay! Quit yer bellyachin'," Sallie feels it is time for him to give some soothing advice. "Everything is beginnin' to look up for you."

Even the Clown knows he is bein' suckered now. "What's lookin' up for me? A coupla days ago I was a slightly depressed person. You come along an' help me out an' now I am like a man without a country."

"There is just no satisfyin' you, is there, Joey? You come to me with a problem. I go to bat for you an' the bottom line is that you do not have a problem anymore."

"I do not have a problem anymore," the Clown is now nodding in agreement. "Salvatore, not only don't I got a problem anymore – I don't got nothin' anymore!"

"Ya got cannoli, Joey, an' it is fresh." Fats is standin' next to the Clown, holdin' a plate filled with cannoli, showin' much tenderness for Joey's misery. We are all pretty much in awe over the actions of Fats

Suozzo because such a sacrifice on his part is hard to believe. "Vito just drops it off here this mornin'. I am sure if ya have some it'll make ya feel a lot better." He holds a custard-filled pastry out to the Clown, who looks at it for a few seconds, then with no reluctance at all, takes it an' gulps it down in one big swallow, grinnin' as the pastry cream dribbles down his chin. It is fortunate that the Clown's attention span is such that a little sweetness is able to make him forget all the bitterness so quickly. We jus' stand there smilin' a little an' doin' some snifflin' like we just watch a four-kleenex movie while the Clown is now busily diggin' away at his third cannoli an' there is the slight possibility that Fats Suozzo is maybe regrettin' a little bit that he is such a caring human being.

Unknown to us at the time is that while the Clown is losin' his home, an' everything that goes with it, Louie the Louse is in the process of embarkin' on a journey to gain a new home. He an' Fivel respectively lurk an' slink their way to Penn Station early the next mornin', bein' very careful that they are seen by no one. This is not too difficult an achievement as it is a time of day rarely seen by any of us. If ya told us such a time of day did not exist, you would not get a very great argument. Naturally, there is a slight chance that they could be seen by the milkman but as he merchandises a product never purchased by either Fivel or Louie, he would not know them from the lamp-post – as a matter of fact, he would recognize the lamp-post a lot quicker, not that the lamp-post is a customer, but he sees it every day.

When they get to Penn Station, Fivel has bigger bags under his eyes than Louie the Louse carries onto the train. One may assume that he does not get a good night's sleep lately which is a good assumption because there is no way he can convince Louie the Louse to leave his vest with him. He stays awake at night tryin' to think up different reasons without causin' Louie to get too suspicious. But nothin' works. When he tells Louie that his sister Flossie has no closet space for winter clothes, of which all outerwear is in such category, Louie lets him know that he does not hang his vest in any closet as he wears it to bed, which saves him a good deal of bread as he does not spend on P.J.'s. So it is a most nervous an' distraught Fivel that arrives at Penn Station as he knows his whole plan goes fizz along with the ten G's if he is unable to produce Louie the Louse's vest as proof that the deed is done. That the deed will not be done anyhow does not enter into the picture. Fivel is so desperate that he thinks if maybe he gets an affidavit signed by a Notary Public sayin' that he blows away Louie the Louse, this will be accepted by the Dwarf instead of Louie's vest or Louie's head. An' maybe Santa Claus will climb down Fivel's chimney on Christmas Eve an' deposit the ten G's in his stockin'. Is it any wonder that Fivel Finnegan finds it so hard to believe that he is born inta such a cruel world?

But when it comes to latchin' onto the green, whether by hook or by crook or whatever scheme a devious mind can come up with, there is no quit in Fivel Finnegan. So it is that together with all the fare-thee-wells, adieus an' ciaos, Fivel pulls out a brand new Kodak he has just purchased at Macy's, of whom he is a devoted customer due to their very liberal return-with-money-back policy, an' tells Louie the Louse to pose for a partin' snapshot. This is an experience which Louie is not greatly acquainted with. Outside of the boys at the local precinct he can think of no other person who ever requests a picture of him. It is said that his mother once has a baby portrait done of Little Louie sittin' on a pony when a studio photographer takes a freebie promotional picture of him. When the photograph is developed the pony, who somehow snatches a quick glance, starts foaming at the mouth, Louie's mother faints away an' the photographer immediately embarks on a career change. Needless to say, the picture no longer exists, nor does the negative – as to the photographer, no one really knows.

So it is no wonder that Louie asks, "Whaddya wanna a pitcher of me for? Ya gonna hang it next to yer bed?"

Fivel tries to make very light of the question by sayin', "It's nice to have pictures of yer friends."

Louie the Louse shrugs, "If ya say so. I wouldn't know. I never had no friend so I never had no pitcher of no friend." As there is always somethin' resemblin' a smile plastered on Louie's face, Fivel does not have to ask him to say 'cheese' – he just aims the camera an' shoots.

Louie is surprised. "Is that it?"

"That is it," Fivel answers. "All done."

"I dunno." It is like Louie the Louse is a little confused. "The other times I have my pitcher taken it is always three shots – front, right profile, left profile an' then I get my fingers inked for prints. I guess you are just not very professional."

Fivel does not choose to argue or debate that statement as it is of very little importance to him. What is important is that he now will have a picture of Louie the Louse which will include his face, his hair, his hands, his feet, his pants and his vest. The cost of buyin' color film did not exactly thrill Fivel but he chalks it up as a very worthwhile investment. So, with a heart filled with hope an' a camera filled with film, Fivel sends Louie the Louse on his way with last minute instructions about not jumpin' in to do anything until he becomes familiar with the town an' keepin' a low profile so nobody knows where he is. Louie's great concern, in fact, Louie's only concern is that Flossie is a good cook. The train hardly chugs its way outta Penn Station when Fivel Finnegan runs over to the nearest telephone booth an' tears out the pages listin' "Tailors" from the Brooklyn telephone book.

At this time I am of the opinion that the Dwarf is accumulatin' quite a nice little bundle in his own backyard. In truth, it takes an awful lotta nickels to build into a substantial number but the way Joey the Clown is droppin' buffaloes inta the Wurlitzer jukebox in the Club it may not take too long before the Dwarf can consider early retirement. One of the boys drops a nickel in the jukebox one day an', without lookin', presses a button an' on comes Sophie Tucker beltin' out what becomes Joey's theme song, "Some Of These Days". To the rest of us it becomes cruel an' inhuman punishment. In fact, Foghorn Manganaro tries to push through a rule that there can be no more Russian Roulette type of record selections. Joey the Clown, Coney Island's homely, homeless version of Casanova is playin' this song all day an' all night every day of the week since Big Nose Sallie solves his problem an' rids him of Angie an' Goldie in one shot. Every one of us walk aroun', inside the Club an' outside, hummin' an' singin' the words even though we get to hate the sound of this song. An' if by chance Joey does run out of nickels it is an even worse situation because then, instead of Sophie T invadin' our sensitivities with style, we walk in on what I can best describe as the remains of Joey the Clown, whose head would be restin' on the counter while he is somewhere in between wailin' an' moanin'

"Some of these days you'll miss me, honey

Some of these days you'll feel so lonely

You'll miss my huggin'

You'll miss my kissin'

You'll miss me, honey,

When you're away."

It is not definite in our minds who causes such melancholy for the Clown, Angie or Goldie, but all of us bein' bettin' men of long standin', I can say with a good deal of assurance, nobody's money would be ridin' on Angie. What does not make the Clown feel any better is a call he gets from Goldie tellin' him she is leavin' town as she gets a job which she thinks will help her grow as a person an' it will give both of them time to think things over. This does not sit too well with the Clown at all as thinkin' is simply not his style.

When Goldie leaves Junior's she is not bein' exactly weighed down by her bankbook an' she is a wise enough doll to realize if she wishes to continue enjoyin' such everyday pleasures as food she must find other employment post haste. She also feels it is important that such other employment not be too nearby in order for her to properly work things out in her head about the Clown an' herself. So, what she does is draft what is called a resume` which she brings to a printer an' has copies sent to restaurants an' such in several large cities like Chicago, Boston, Philadelphia an' Miami. Bein' neither a poet nor a dramatist, Goldie gets right to the point relatin' her credentials – "Although I can do many things I have been pretty much a specialist for the past year, serving up cheesecake and I can honestly say that nobody is better in the cheesecake department than I am." Along with this autobiographical masterpiece she sends her snapshot, which in Goldie's case can never hurt her unless she is applyin' for the position of Mother Superior in a convent.

Less than a week goes by when she gets a call from this place, "Sweet Stuff" in Miami Beach, offerin' her a job.

Although Joey is not too happy when Goldie calls him with this news, Goldie is not overjoyed herself mostly because she does not know of Joey's unhappiness. Actually, while she is on the train to Miami she is beginnin' to have second thoughts about what she is doin', especially since she asks Joey if he wants to have a sort of farewell dinner with her an' he begs off, sayin' he has no clean clothes to go out in. She cannot decide whether it is one very stupid or one very creative excuse and figures he is probably in love with the idea of havin' his freedom. It is not exactly the game plan Goldie had in mind as it is much easier playin' a hard to get doll when the party of the second part is a little bit grief-stricken. She does not mean the Clown has to do a Steve Brodie off the Brooklyn Bridge but a little pain would be a very comfortin' thing to see. It is still not very clear in Goldie's mind whether what she is doin' is selfish or noble – that is, she is not too sure whether she is sufferin' from cold feet or is sacrificin' herself on account of she is not worthy of a Joey DiCollonna. Maybe she should not be so noble by leaving the Clown to mankind like Big Nose Sallie feels she should. Joey may not be the greatest catch in the world, but he is a catch.

While Goldie is headin' South wishin' she had stayed up North, Fivel Finnegan, who does not wish to blow a major chunk of his soon-to-be ten G's on taxi fares goin' from tailor to tailor, makes a cut-rate deal with the Widder Brown. It is a deal he is soon wishin' he never makes because it is beginnin' to look like there is a pretty good chance he does not live to see his money. He is directin' her all over Brooklyn an' is beginnin' to feel like a German Shepherd. It is not even rewarding when she tells him that driving down McDonald Avenue, dodging the el pillars, is maybe the most fun she ever had. About a dozen silent prayers later Fivel finds a tailor named Max on Flatbush Avenue who squints at Fivel's picture of Louie the Louse and announces that he can duplicate such a vest but can't believe anyone would want to wear it. Fivel is so happy, he does not even bargain on the price, which upsets him very much when he realizes what he has done.

When Fivel leaves Max's Tailor Shop and gets back into the Widder Brown's cab, Minnie says to him, "I never seen anyone go to so many tailors. What're you doin', comparison shopping, Fivel?"

"Proper attire is the mark of a true gentleman, Minnie. One cannot be too careful in the selection of the right tailor."

"Is that a fact?" If Minnie Brown is not genuinely surprised at such a pronoucement, she does not show it. "And here I was, always under the impression that you cannot tell a book by its cover."

For Fivel, life is becomin' more precious with every passin' minute an' that is because as soon as Max is finished with the vest, which he says will be in two or three days, Fivel will present the vest to the Dwarf an' then live happily ever after as a person of means. This makes Fivel very nervous over the way the Widder Brown drives, because, God forbid there is a bad accident now ... before, so what, he is just another poor slob who gets counted out; but, now, what a pity it would be, just when he has everything to live for – Zap! Suddenly, Fivel realizes that Fame an' Fortune carry a hefty price tag. It is a real dilemma when you cannot afford to get yourself killed an' you find you are bein' driven around town by the Widder Brown. With this realization, as Minnie is drivin' under the el like it is a slalom course in the Alps, Fivel croaks, "Minnie, please look at the way you are drivin'!"

"If I could do that," she answers with a big lop-sided, gap-toothed grin, "I would be able to drive all over the city without one of you guys bein' my co-pilot. Ya sure do expect a lot from a blind, old lady."

Fivel sees this picture flash in front of him of his two sisters all dolled up in mink coats, carryin' patent leather pocket books stuffed with the dough they inherit from their lovin' brother who had the poor misfortune of never bein' able to enjoy his ten G's as he winds up splattered all over some street in Brooklyn, New York, U.S.A.

"Maybe I should get out an' walk the rest of the way as it is such a lovely night for walkin'," Fivel sputters.

"An' leave me lost in a place that I do not even know an' cannot see an' even if I could see I probably wouldn't know where it is," a horrified

Widder Brown answers. "Fivel Finnegan, you are no gentleman an' if you try to leave me here, you never will have the opportunity to ever become one." Fivel, recognizing there are more ways than one to meet your end, wisely decides to remain in the cab, and as always, Minnie Brown safely negotiates her hack back to its roosting place in Coney Island where Fivel climbs out on legs that are flip-floppin' like soggy spaghetti an' somehow manages to stagger into the Mermaid S.A.C. lookin' like the only survivor after Chief Sitting Bull an' his brave braves do their number at Little Big Horn.

There are only a few of us in the Club at this time an' we do not believe the shape Fivel is in. If we are told he just finishes takin' a ride with the Widder Brown, then we would understand his condition but we are not privy to such information so all we do is stare an' gawk until Joey the Clown speaks up. "Not that ya ever look too good, Fivel, but the truth is, I have seen ya look better."

Like I said, when it comes to latchin' onto the green, there is no quit in Fivel Finnegan an' in such situations his brain runs on all cylinders so he does not tell us about his ride but, instead, uses the shape he is in to his fullest advantage. Moppin' his brow, he plops himself down on a stool by the counter an' lookin' up at us, says, "It is done, guys. The deed is done." Nobody says a word. We just stare at him, waitin' for a little more detailed description of what deed is done so Fivel goes on, "It is not easy for a guy with my intellect an' sensitive disposition, whose natural bent is for supervisory an' administrative work, but I have upheld my committment an' the honor of our esteemed leader, Donato Langella, by riddin' the world of Louie the Louse. That is why I am in the condition in which you see me. I am not accustomed to performin' such a job."

It is understandable that at this moment we are all truly impressed. Fats Suozzo even gets hold of some scrap paper an' asks Fivel for his autograph, only Fivel's hand is still shakin' too much to oblige. "Wow! Tell us how ya did it, Fivel?" Fats asks an' it looks like his eyes are poppin' outta their sockets. "See, I told all of ya not to worry, that Fivel was the real thing."

Fivel, now seein' that he has center stage an' not exactly dislikin' it, holds up his hands to keep his audience in check. "Hold it, guys! Where is the Dwarf an' Big Nose Sallie?"

"Hey! That is right!" Fats exclaims, "Fivel got ten G's comin' to him. They are not here just yet, Fivel. Boy, the boss'll be real proud of ya."

It is then that the Clown interrupts, "Yeah, but he ain't gonna pay off without proof. He is gonna wanna see the corpse's delicatessen."

"As the job I have performed," Fivel explains, "is of such a thorough nature, what is left of Louie the Louse would make ashes an' dust seem like a block of granite. So, instead of a corpus delecti, I will be presentin' to the Dwarf the very distinguishable vest of our late, departed friend." There then commences to be much back-slappin' an' congratulations for Fivel, who never before has been thought of as a hero an' no matter how much plastic surgery he may undertake, he will never, never look the part.

"Why ain't the vest here now?" Foghorn Manganaro wants to know.

"Ya think I would give one of you wisenheimers the chance to filch it from me?" Fivel answers. "Oh, no. I am gonna bring it in here when I know the Dwarf is here an' we will have a combination wake an' celebration."

Fivel is not the only one with the ability to take advantage of such a moment. Of course, ya must understand that all things are relative. Fats, seeing the chance to capitalize on this situation in a way that, to him, is almost as excitin' an rewardin' as Fivel's good fortune, pounces on him an' advises, "Such an occassion gotta be catered. Ya know that, don't ya, Fivel?"

"Yer kiddin' me!" Fivel says with surprise. "Who ever heard of such a thing?"

"Oh, this is a very major event, Fivel," Fats explains. "You have rid the world of a terrible villain and you have given us our independence. I mean, that calls for a real big celebration. It gotta be catered."

"I don't think it is appropriate." Fivel is quite perplexed right now. "It's just a wake ..."

"No! No!" Fats cuts in. "What you have done has brought peace to us. That always calls for a caterer."

"It does?"

"Whaddya think happened when the Pilgrims whip the bad Indians an' make peace with the good ones?"

Fivel just shakes his head.

"They had this big celebration which was catered," Fats tells him. "Ya never heard of Thanksgiving?"

"Yeah. Sure I did," Fivel answers, "but is that the same as ..."

"Of course it is," Fats cuts in again, "an' it was catered. Turkey, cranberry sauce, sweet potatos, all the trimmin's. An' what about when we annihilate the British, who useta be as bad as Louie the Louse. Wasn't that the same kinda celebration as we're gonna have?"

"That was catered, too?" Fivel is a little embarrassed at the education he is gettin'.

"Independence Day!" Fats bellows. "Hot dogs, hamburgers, potato salad – of course it was catered."

Fivel holds up his hands in an effort to stop Fats, who is now droolin' in anticipation. "We are talkin' about somewhat different things. What we have here is a simple rubout, not a history class. Who ever heard of catering ..."

"Ho! Ho! Ho!" Fats almost pounces on Fivel an' his Ho! Ho! Ho! sounds sorta like 'Checkmate'. "A simple rubout? Ya ever hear of the Valentine's Day Massacre – ya know, the Purple Gang – Bang! Bang!"

Fivel, who is not too often flustered, is now. "Sure, I know about ... ya mean that's catered, too?"

Fats turns on this very condescending look. "I don't believe it. An intelligent man like you. Of course it's catered – a box of candy, candlelight dinners. Don't ya see, Fivel? Ya got no choice. You have done somethin' bigger than yerself. It gotta be catered." Fivel just shakes his head in – I don't know what you'd call it – victory or defeat. Actually, we were all very happy as we have not had a nice party, especially a catered one, in a long time.

CHAPTER FIFTEEN

'SWEET STUFF'

I always enjoy a party. It don't matter what kinda party – birthday party, victory party, New Year's Eve party – a party's a party. It gives you a chance to spiff up with your Sunday best, splash on a gallon of Bay Rum, get a real good spit shine on your shoes an' let off all your pent-up steam. The fact that you are generally struttin' your stuff in front of a roomful of made-up dolls does not detract from the situation. All the guys feel pretty much the same way as I do, which is not really surprisin'. What is surprisin' is that Joey the Clown is not sharin' in this festive mood. Usually, Joey is the biggest party animal around. Probably because of all the free eats that goes along with it. But this time Joey is very much down at the mouth. It is true that he is a most depressed Clown right now by virtue of bein' divested of both his women, but Joey is very good at compartmentalisin' things in his life. He is not the kinda guy who mixes good an' bad together an' comes out with a diluted mixture. No, Joey is the kinda guy who has this unique ability to shove bad completely aside when somethin' good comes along an' really enjoy the good like there never was anything bad, an' when he's finished with the good then he goes back to the bad a hundred per cent just like there never was any good. But like I said, this time it is different. It is like the party does not pick him up at all.

Finally, though I do not usually intrude on one's privacy, I say to him, "Joey, you are not yourself." To which he responds in a fashion very typical of Joey the Clown. "Right now I do not mind bein' someone else but it really don't help whether I am someone else or myself because no matter who I am, I ain't got no clean clothes. An' if I do not have any clean clothes I cannot go to no party which is also alright as I am in no mood to go to no party."

There is no chance in the world I am goin' to ask Joey to repeat what he says. "Instead of feelin' sorry for yourself, whaddya do when your clothes need to be cleaned an' pressed?" I ask him.

He shrugs his shoulders. "Ya know, I ain't too up on that, Sonny. Angie always took care of things like that. I had alla my work to do an' little things like that she took care of. I jus' put them in the hamper an' a few days later they are hangin' in my closet all clean."

"Then all ya gotta do, Joey," I say to him with a big smile as I am definitely makin' headway, "is get your clothes together an' bring 'em to the Dry Cleaners where they will be cleaned an' pressed so then ya can go to the party an' have a good time."

"Hey, yeah," the realization dawns on him, "I'm pretty sure that's exactly what Angie used to do."

"Ain't no other way, Joey," I clue him in.

It is obviously a great relief to Joey as for the first time in a while there is a smile on his face. "I am gonna go get my clothes outta the hamper right now."

It is then that I know it is not gonna be as easy as I thought. "Hamper? What hamper, Joey?" My question is a very reasonable one, as like most Social Athletic Clubs, a hamper was not included in our furniture inventory.

"Oh, you know, Sonny," now he is clueing' me in. "The big hamper at the side of the buildin'."

I do not remember if it is Laurel an' Hardy or maybe the Marx Brothers, but in this movie I saw a while ago I am laughin' so hard I am ready to pee in my pants because someone on an ocean liner is throwin' his clothes out the porthole which he thinks is a hamper or laundry chute. What makes it so funny I tell myself is that it is some-thin' that can never happen in real life. If I ever see that movie again I will probably not laugh next time.

Though I do not wish to go on with Joey's education, I have no choice. "Joey, that big hamper is not a hamper. It is a dumpster, a gar-bage container an' this mornin' was a pick-up day, Joey."

I am not gonna relate what Joey does or says at that time because if I just make mention of the fact that he has experienced more cheerful mo-ments it would not be any more of an understatement. It is only when I point out to him that this is not just a party but the celebration of maybe the most momentous as well as unbelievable occassion to ever affect us personally, that Joey agrees to join in, even if it means gettin' new threads.

It is sorta like things are beginnin' to look up a bit for Joey when Foghorn walks in with the Daily News which, when he drops it down on the counter next to Joey, is opened up to a full page ad for a super one-day sale at Ripley Brothers. Joey is feelin' like this is almost Divine intervention as he grabs up the paper an' heads for the door, yellin' back at me, "When I come back you will think I am Cinderella after she goes shoppin' with her Fairy Godmother!" Joey ain't too much of a reader.

He runs down the block to Widder Brown's cab, hops in the back an' says, "I know it is outta yer area, but it is urgent that I get to Ripley's, so I will direct ya very carefully an' you will drive very carefully." To which Minnie responds, "I always drive carefully, but you bring out the worst in me with your directions, Joseph DiCollonna. Ya think it was easy tellin' the Judge that a lotta people confuse the boardwalk with the Brooklyn Bridge?"

"I told ya, I am really sorry about that one, Minnie. If I wouldn'ta forgot my watch that mornin' it never woulda happened," Joey is most apologetic as well as more than a little sheepish. "When we get to Ocean Parkway I know I turn in the direction of where my watch is, which is my left hand, which I look at, but seein' only a bare wrist I tell ya to turn right an' we wind up on the boardwalk. But I am a man about it, Minnie. I take full responsibility in fronta the judge. Anyhow, probation ain't so bad."

"What time is it, Joey?" Widder Brown asks.

"It is ten after ...," Joey starts, but is interrupted immediately by Minnie. "That's okay, Joey, I just wanted to make sure you was wearin' your watch now before you start givin' directions. Where'd you say you wanted to go to, again?"

"Ripley's", Joey holds up the Daily News as if Minnie could read it. "Foghorn Manganaro jus' walks in with this newspaper showin' this big sale at Ripley's only for today an' me needin' a new suit worse'n ..."

"Forget it," Minnie interrupts him again. "Foghorn just buys that paper from me less than a half hour ago an' you know at my bargain rate of two cents you should only read about sales that say 'tomorrow', not 'today'."

"Your paper?" It is all that can come outta Joey's mouth.

"Look at the bright side of it, Joey," Widder Brown says with a smile, "which is all the money I have just saved ya."

"Yeah? Tell me that when ya come to visit me at the nudist colony because pretty soon I ain't gonna have no choice but to live there."

"Ya mean Angie ran off with your clothes?" a shocked Widder Brown asks.

"Nah," Joey answers, "it wasn't Angie. It was the garbage man."

"Tsk! Tsk!" Minnie just shakes her head like she is not believin' what she hears. "What kinda world is it where ya cannot trust your own garbage man?" Just then she snaps up an' turns around to Joey in a most excited manner. "Why didn't I think about it before? If it is clothes that you need, I just recently finish takin' Fivel Finnegan on a comparison shoppin' tour of all the tailors in Brooklyn an' he narrows it down to what I am sure must be the very best, an' if chosen by Fivel, the cheapest tailor around."

This immediately perks up Joey the Clown, who asks, "Do ya know where this guy is?"

"I can never forget," sighs the Widder Brown, "because it was such an exciting ride. He is on Flatbush Avenue but if I take ya there we gotta go with McDonald Avenue an' drive under the el."

"But, Minnie," Joey points out, "if we go that way I gotta direct you around all those pillars!"

It is not easy to imagine Minnie Brown with the smile of an angel but that is exactly how she is lookin' at this moment. "I know."

Max the Tailor does not know what to think when he sees this snag-toothed hag wearin' a hack-driver's cap carry this shapeless heap into his shop.

"Is he dead?" Max croaks.

"Not yet," Minnie answers. "Maybe on the drive back. Right now, he has only fainted."

Obviously, Minnie's magic is not too powerful because it takes only a few splashes of cold water to bring Joey the Clown back to the real world.

A couple days later Goldie is not feelin' nearly as low as when she was on the train an' that is because Joey calls her the previous night to see how she is doin' an also he invites her to a very big party – a catered party, no less – bein' thrown by Fivel Finnegan celebratin' his riddin' the world of Louie the Louse. Goldie finds this very hard to believe – scrawny little Fivel, a cold-blooded killer! Joey tells her how he even sees Louie's vest hanging up in the tailor shop that Fivel goes to and that it is obvious he is having it cleaned before presenting it to the Dwarf and collecting a big reward. To Goldie it seems like an awful lot is happen-ing back home. Even though it is geographically impossible for her to go to the party, Joey's invitin' her makes her feel real good. Maybe Joey is not so in love with having his freedom after all. At least not so much that he does not think about her. It puts Goldie in the kinda mood that – well, if I am in such a mood I would have my hands in my pockets an' I would be whistlin' away like Al Jolson; if Fats is in such a mood we would soon be in a custardless world an' if it is Joey the Clown in such a mood we would have a Fatsless world because no way would Joey let Fats get away with all that custard – but what it does to Goldie is make her bounce along Collins Avenue with her fanny swishin' left to right like it is on a rubber band which causes many pedestrians an' strollers to think all the traffic lights are red in every direction because all traf-fic comes to an absolute an' complete halt. There is a traffic cop on the corner but he is of no help once he swallows his whistle an' pretty soon the pedestrians are no longer thinkin' about traffic lights because they are too busy figurin' out ways to keep from bumpin' into one another while they walk in one direction but their eyes are travelin' in another direction – viewin' the rotation of Goldie's rump.

It is very fortunate that Goldie, who is slightly lost, is not lost for very long because the traffic in Miami Beach would be backed up to Tallahassee if she does not remove herself from view. She finds the "Sweet Stuff" on Collins Avenue directly opposite the Roney Plaza an' from the outside it does not resemble any pastry shop or restaurant she has ever seen before but Goldie knows that a creative mind can think up some pretty novel ways to serve cheesecake 'n coffee.

Once she is inside it does not take her eyes too long to adjust to the dark, probably because Goldie is very big on nibblin' on carrots. As soon as she is able to see she makes her way to the large horseshoe bar in the center where three guys are sittin' an' asks, with as much authority in her voice as she can muster up, "Who's in charge here?" To which the first guy points to the second, the second guy points to the third who points back to the first an' all of them say together, "He is."

As soon as they are convinced that Goldie is not in the employ of the F.B.I., the Treasury Department or the Miami Beach Police Department, all fingers turn an' point to the second guy, Foxie Molloy, who owns up to it with an "I am. And you must be Goldie, our new employee whose picture, I must say, does not do you justice. Also, it is not a usual practice for me to hire anyone from fifteen hundred miles away but your letter – what a piece of work. You really got a way with words, Goldie, ya know? 'I am a specialist in servin' up cheesecake' and 'no one is better in the cheesecake department than I am'. I never had a doll who could double as a comic before. You are somethin' else again."

"Do not think that I am lacking in humility," Goldie explains, "it is just that I believe if you do something well you should not be ashamed to let the world know."

"No sense hidin' it," Foxie laughs. "But ya do tease the customers a little bit first, don't ya? Look at me askin' such dumb questions to a real pro!"

This question makes Goldie hesitate for a minute. "I have been trained to give my customers what they are paying for as quick as possible. They come in, sit down and I am right on top of them. That's the way they like it."

Foxie is now goggle-eyed an' he is actin' like his collar, which is already open at the neck, is way too tight. "Wow! I only hope you are not throwin' too much at them.   Maybe ya go a little easier on our crowd ... at least till they get used to it."

"I always believe in giving a healthy serving. If what you are dishing out is quality the customer will always be back for more. But if you want me to cut down a little bit, I am at your disposal." Which remark makes Foxie Molloy one very red-faced and aroused individual who croaks, "You are? Well, why don't ya give me an' the boys a little sample of your routine. I am sure you are most excitin' to watch but just give us a little taste."

There is no question that this request confuses Goldie somewhat. She cannot imagine what is so important about Foxie eating his own cheesecake but after thinking it over for a few seconds, she says, "I will need a spatula and some plates." At which Foxie turns to his two buddies an' gives with one of those really sly winks, "We are gonna see it done a little differently, I think, guys. You know, real high class New York style. Maybe with a little S-M thrown in, huh?" While he is talkin', he is already bouncin' off to the kitchen from where he returns almost immediately with the spatula an' plates. "Go to it, Goldie baby."

"Let me see your cheesecake," Goldie smiles innocently.

Foxie almost doubles over in convulsions, laughin' so hard, the tears are squirtin' outta his eyes. "What an act! You are funnier than Gracie Allen. You let us see your cheesecake." Now Goldie is gettin' just a little apprehensive, hoping there is no misunderstanding. "I thought I made it very plain in my resum'e; I only serve, I do not bake."

"Maybe you do not bake," Foxie roars, wipin' his eyes, then blowin' his nose before he can continue talkin', "but in my book you are cookin' with gas, baby! Enough, though, with the schtick! It is obvious you can go on forever but I do not have forever as I want you on for tonight so let us glimpse the merchandise now, Goldie ... Do you have a G-string with you?"

"Why? Is your guitar broken?" Goldie cannot keep up with the strange requests comin' outta Mister Foxie Molloy.

"Is my guitar broken?" Foxie Molloy cannot keep up with the wise-acre comebacks shootin' outta this doll Goldie. "I do not play a musical instrument of any kind an' also, I do not run a jerkwater operation. You will have a four-piece combo accompanyin' you through your routine."

"That seems very extravagant to me," Goldie replies in true admiration. "At Junior's the only time I had music accompanying me or any of the other girls was if the busboy would be whistling while clearing the tables."

"Oh, not here, Goldie. It is my philosophy that the music is most important," Foxie emphasizes. "I am right now picturin' in my mind you strippin' off all your clothes to an 'Off to Buffalo.'" It is almost simultaneous with the utterance of such remark that Foxie Molloy's face becomes embellished with the additional adornment of five fingers on its right side, these five fingers bein' a perfect match for the five fingers that happen to belong to Goldie's left hand.

"Whatja do that for?" A shocked Foxie whimpers in disbelief, cuppin' his burning cheek tenderly with his hand. "We can change the music. It don't have to be an 'Off to Buffalo'. I mean, it ain't carved in stone, ya know ... Hey, where ya goin', Goldie?" He now jumps up as Goldie is bee-linin' for the door.

"I am doing what you would call an 'Off to Hoboken'," Goldie cries. "You have deceived me, Mr. Foxie Molloy. My friend Gertie Gutenyu of show biz fame had to serve cocktails in a very short tu-tu. Being a progressive, broad-minded modern woman, I can accept that. But to serve cheesecake in the raw – yech! There is something very sick about your mind and I am serving notice immediately. I do not suppose there would be any severance pay involved, would there?"

"Just a second, Goldie," Foxie orders, holding up his hand for attention, "you cannot just walk outta here like that. I have invested in you the fare to bring ya down here. You have a commitment to honor."

"I will repay you the money as soon as I get back home," Goldie promises.

"What you are perpetrating is an unfair labor practice," Foxie warns. "Are you familiar with the Taft-Hartley Act?"

"Of course I am," Goldie bluffs, wonderin' to herself if it was anything like the Abbot and Costello "Who's On First" Act.

"You are?" This causes Foxie to hesitate for a minute. "On second thought, let us not deal with legal technicalities. Instead, I will turn this over to my newly retained Business and Insurance Protective Agency. Louie, here is your first assignment." He turns towards his two bar companions who are hidden away at the dimly lighted bar. The one he beckons to stands up an' he becomes much more visible with his red plaid vest. For some reason there is somethin' resemblin' a smile plastered on his face. "There is no way I can permit my client's contract to be broken."

Goldie does not move. She stands with her mouth hangin' open like a steam shovel ready to scoop up its load an' her eyes look like they are standin' out on antennas. No words come outta her. As Louie gets closer an' is able to see her in the light he stops an' does a double-take. "As I live an' breathe, Joey the Clown's girl, Goldie."

"Wrong."

"You are not Goldie?" he asks with great surprise.

"That part is right," she answers. "What is wrong is that you 'live and breathe'. You happen to be dead and your wake is the day after tomorrow."

CHAPTER SIXTEEN

A CATERED WAKE

What I remember most about Louie the Louse's wake is that I have seen wakes at which there was more cryin'. Louie's wake was different. I cannot explain but it was more like ... well, more like a Chinese New Year celebration. Ya gotta hand it to Fivel, the little guy pulled out all the stoppers; he spared nothin'. It is true, he was advised by Fats Suozzo an' I gotta admit, nobody is more creative than Fats when it comes to fillin' a room with food but, still, it was Fivel who opens his pocketbook. I am sure he gets a big break from Vito Fusillo but when ya use a class outfit like the Villa Vito as your caterer you are goin' with the best so it cannot be too cheap. And to add that extra special touch, at Fats' suggestion Vito has Juniors deliver their cheesecake for dessert. "Without question, a wake to die for," Fats sighed. The Mermaid Social Athletic Club is decked out an' spruced up so good that even our old ladies, who are invited to pay their respects an' partake in such a joyous occassion, got no gripes or complaints about the place.

Ya know this is a big, big event for us because even Big Nose Sallie becomes involved in organizin' the evening. It is his suggestion that we all get there early and then Fivel Finnegan arrives to make a grand entrance. Sallie even sets up a dress code – that is how momentous this

wake is. When Fivel enters the Club, we are the best fed and most sar-
torially resplendent group of mourners ya ever laid eyes on.

Although one would think that Fivel would be overjoyed upon makin' his entrance, that is not exactly the way it is. In fact, he does not
touch any of the food an' he just stands an' stares, like he is a pillar of
salt. Draped over his forearm is the red plaid vest that he is to trade in
for his ten G's. The fact that Fivel Finnegan is not as happy as he should
be does not escape any of us, even though we are each industriously
involved in hopping from the lobster to the calamari to the lasagna an'
right on down the buffet line. Finally, Fats cannot bear to see such a sad
face on such a joyful night, so he walks up to Fivel, balancing a platter of food on his left hand an' pats Fivel on the shoulder with his right
hand, saying, "C'mon, have some food. Put a smile on your face. You
are actin' like you are at a wake."

Meanwhile, I am sayin' to myself how Fats looks even fatter in his
red plaid vest. It is somethin' he should never wear. Not that I like how
I look in mine ... in fact, none of the guys look good in their red plaid
vests because it is just too loud for my taste. But that is what Big Nose
Sallie selects for the dress code an' bein' that he springs for the vests,
who are we to say 'no'. I mean, even if he wouldn'ta made them gifts,
we do not say 'no' to Big Nose Sallie. I am also more than a little certain that the reason Fivel Finnegan has no appetite has more than just a
little to do with this dress code. The first thing he sees when he walks
into the Club is a roomful of guys wearin' red plaid vests which immediately makes the vest he is carryin' over his arm not such a standout as
it mighta been.

All along, Big Nose Sallie has a problem believin' that Fivel does
a number on Louie the Louse. Not that the rest of us lap it up. It is
just that our minds do not linger on a proposition the way Sallie's does.
Sallie said from the beginnin' that to get the ten G's there hadda be proof
positive or in the words of Joey the Clown, the corpse's delicatessen.
But the Dwarf sets up the ground rules which say that Louie the Louse's
vest will be accepted in place of the corpus delectus so that is how the
game is played. Only Big Nose Sallie makes himself the self-appointed

umpire an' he is gonna make sure that the rules do not get bent outta shape. From the first time Fivel suggests that Louie may wind up somethin' like sawdust an' that's why there should be some substitute proof of his rubout, Sallie smells limburger cheese. He spends so much time pacin' the floor an' scratchin' his head to stimulate his thinkin' that it begins to look like maybe he has developed a major dandruff condition.

So when Joey the Clown calls Goldie in Miami Beach, which he does from the Mermaid S.A.C., to tell her about Louie the Louse's wake, although Big Nose Sallie is not an eavesdropper, he cannot help but pay very close attention to what Joey says about seein' Louie's red plaid vest hangin' in a tailor shop. For Salvatore Pignasale the trail does not have to get any warmer than this. No sooner does the Clown hang up the telephone that he finds the arm of Big Nose Sallie draped around his shoulder in a display of warmth an' comraderie that one does not usually expect from such a person. And it is at the request of Sallie that these two bosom buddies engage the services of the Widder Brown so that he can give his approval of what Joey orders from Max the Tailor for the big, upcoming catered wake. Big Nose Sallie finds it to be very strange that the Clown keeps his eyes tightly closed for the entire drive while he chomps away at his fingernails like they are corn-on-the-cob but as there are more important considerations on Sallie's mind just now he does not bother discussin' this ritual with Joey.

When Big Nose Sallie sees the red plaid vest hangin' in the shop of Max the Tailor he does not automatically assume, as the Clown does, that it is the hand-me-down vest from Knuckles McTavish to Louie the Louse which Fivel Finnegan is havin' cleaned before presentin' to the Dwarf. One reason Sallie is the Dwarf's right hand man and chief adviser is that he does not assume anything an' he questions everything. It is obvious when he asks Max about the vest that Max has been induced to remain most silent on this topic. Therefore, Sallie, convincing negotiator that he is, simply makes stronger inducements that are most advantageous to Max the Tailor, pot-sweeteners such as Max continuing to live out his life, this bein' the major inducement, and a financial bonanza wherein Big Nose Sallie places an order with Max to increase the number of vests he is makin' from one to a dozen. He then impresses on Max the importance of sayin' absolutely nothing to Fivel about this transaction when he comes in to pick up his vest. Sallie explains that if there is any doubt in Max's mind about his ability to remain silent now, he can help him out by the surgical removal of his tongue. Max assures Big Nose Sallie that he will forego the surgery as he does not think it would be covered by Blue Cross. Big Nose Sallie feels there may be other reasons for this decision and is most confident that Max the Tailor will be one very quiet person.

So it is no great wonder that at this moment Fivel is feelin' like a person is supposed to feel at a wake. In fact, he couldn't feel any worse if it was his own wake, which may have been a thought not too far removed from Fivel's mind. To everyone else the red plaid vests were pretty much like costumes at a dress-up party. Only Fivel Finnegan an' Big Nose Sallie knew the message they were sending. What compounds Fivel's depression is that he keeps thinkin' how it may turn out that he pays the tab for his own funeral – this from a dude who gets palpitations from payin' the tab for anything. He would like very much to be someplace else right now as he does not feel this is the healthiest environment for him to be in at this time but for the host of such a shindig to be missing, many eyebrows would be raised, some of which are already raised as there is not quite one hundred per cent attendance at this most festive wake which is beginnin' to take on some very somber overtones.

It is not unnatural to assume that Big Nose Sallie gives one vest to every guy that is associated with the Club as Big Nose Sallie is one very fair, even-handed sort of a guy. An' if it turns out that someone does not receive a vest the automatic assumption would be that such a person would be someone who can easily be overlooked – someone who ya do not notice very readily. Although this description does not at all fit the Dwarf, he is the guy that does not get a red plaId vest. Forget the fact that this probably does not break his heart at all. That is strictly beside the point. You may also say, "Well, we are talkin' about an awful lot of material." That is not the way Big Nose Sallie's mind works, sporty guy that he is. Big Nose Sallie's mind plays it very close to the vest, in this instance not a red plaid one. He does not wish to look bad by making a presentation to the Dwarf which will be a very clear message sayin' that a certain debt for a certain eradication job is not due and payable. Sallie knows there is always the chance – a way out long shot, but still a chance - that Fivel, who in Sallie's mind is a cornered weasel, may not go down like an honorable gent but may squawk that he does such a complete job on Louie the Louse that there goes Louie, vest an' all. An', of course, there is always the zillion to one shot that is what happens. So, Sallie is takin' no chances. He has the weasel in a corner, now he waits to see what the weasel does. So far, Fivel Finnegan is not exactly Mr. Giggle-puss.

The fact that the Dwarf does not get a red plaid vest like everyone else is not even known by the rest of the guys because he is not yet in attendance, which is the cause of the raised eyebrows an' starts some talk goin' around the room. This would have been of great concern to Fivel a short while ago when collectin' ten G's was the most important thing on his mind. But at this very moment other things have become much more important to Fivel than money, like seein' tomorrow morning, for instance. An' the likelihood of his seein' tomorrow morning appears much brighter without the Dwarf than with the Dwarf.

But the reason for the Dwarf not bein' at the club yet has nothin' to do with makin' Fivel Finnegan happy or sad. It has much more to do with the fact that even the Dwarf cannot be in two places at the same time and as he is presently at the Coney Island Police Station he is unable to be present at Louie the Louse's wake. It seems that early that morning a telephone call comes into the station-house that makes everybody wish it was his day off. When the desk sergeant answers the call with his usual cheerful greeting of "Hello! If you have a problem why not share it with us?" the caller on the other end of the line begins to share. "I am a disgruntled member of the notorious gang headed by the Dwarf an' as my conscience does not permit me to any longer protect my boss I am now turnin' stool pigeon because it is the American way."

"Did that man litter the sidewalk again?" the desk sergeant asks, hopin' this call comes to a quick end, because bringin' in the Dwarf is somethin' like bringin' in Santa Claus besides which, the Dwarf is very large and cumbersome.

"He has done somethin' even worse," explains Louie. "He has rubbed out one Louis DeLuise, a law-abiding, upstanding citizen who has never brought no harm to no one else."

"I'm sorry, Disgruntled Gang Member, but we are tyin' up the phone. There may be some lost kids out there an' here we are, just talkin' small talk an' passin' the time of day ..."

"Whoa!" Louie cuts in. "I do not wish to go over your head but this guy was lika a brother to me – even closer."

"I have seen no evidence that a crime was committed," the sergeant shoots back.

"Evidence? It is evidence that ya want?" Louie yells so loud into the phone that the sergeant's eyeballs are bumpin' into each other. "Go to the Dwarf's house an' you will find all the evidence you will need. You will find such evidence you will not even need a trial. Ya can execute him right there."

"Well," the sergeant starts backin' off just a drop, "even if we find some evidence that a crime mighta been committed, we still need a witness."

"Ya got one," Louie the Louse snorts. "You bring in the Dwarf an' I will be there to finger him!"

"What is your name again?"

"I told ya – I am a disgruntled gang member," Louie smiles as he hangs up the phone.

No matter how uncomfortable they feel doin' it, the boys at the stationhouse know they cannot take the chance of not checkin' this out. It is not very considerate to bite the hand that feeds you but ya gotta make sure that hand is a little bit clean. When a carload of cops gets to the Dwarf's building a few minutes later they are unable to give a Clean Hands Award because when they walk into the vestibule of the building they almost puke, the janitor is so angry he forgets how to curse in english an' his dog is goin' crazy from happiness. This is because there are bits of bones an' flesh all over the place an' the walls an' terrazzo floor are covered with blood. Scrawled in blood right under the mail boxes was, "the Dwarf killed me ... Louie" an' it trailed off in a smeared line.

Anyhow, that is how the Dwarf winds up gettin' an invitation to the police station where, even though he is treated with more respect than the Police Commissioner, he is still gonna be late for the wake. They are hopin' the Dwarf is not angry but they cannot tell because his face has about as much movement as a wino the morning after he has spent last night locked in a liquor store. It is not too long after Louie's call that the telephone rings again at the stationhouse but this time when the desk sergeant picks it up there is no one on the line because Giuseppe the Butcher's helper changes his mind and decides it does not pay to report a break-in to the police when nothing important was taken. He could not figure who would bother to steal some lamb shanks an' some liver an' beef. Probably some poor hungry tramp.

Just because the Dwarf is not in attendance does not mean his seat remains empty an' unused. If seats could talk I am sure this one would express great pleasure in the unexpected change of occupants that occurs when Goldie comes rushin' into the Club like a storm has hit. In fact, she can be upgraded to one of those hurricanes that come sweepin' up the coast from Florida the way she comes tearin' in here. "Boy! What I got to tell you," she gasps, floppin' into this very happy chair that was expectin' the Dwarf.

I do not believe anyone ever taught the Clown to do cartwheels because I am sure that is what he would have been doing if he knew how to do them. It is obvious he had no idea Goldie was comin' back from Miami just yet. Meanwhile, Fats Suozzo suddenly becomes a very confused and disoriented person when, for the second time in a month, he gets kissed on the mouth; first Fivel an' now the Clown, who is unable to contain his joy an' while Goldie was slightly outta reach, Fats was not. At least with Fivel there was no one around to see it. Fats thinks to himself that maybe it is time for him to change his after-shave lotion.

While Fats is very busy scrubbin' his mouth with the back of his hand and all the guys who are around there very discreetly back away a few steps, the Clown, who right now could be mistaken for a helium-filled balloon the way he is floatin', bounces over to where Goldie is sittin', catchin' her breath an' speaks about the things that are closest to his heart, "Ya won't believe how good the food is. Lemme getcha some ..."

"Joey!" Goldie stops him with a screech. "I got something real important to tell you."

Joey holds his hand out an' shakes it like a traffic cop holdin' back the cars durin' rush hour, points his chin straight ahead an' says, "There is no need to say you are sorry an' admit you made a mistake. It is written all over your face ..."

"Oh, my God!" Goldie panics. "Did my mascara run?" To which Fats Suozzo, who has this ability to hear everything around him, over him an' under him, responds, "I do not recall any nag named My Mascara." He then calls over to Foghorn Manganaro, "Did My Mascara go at Belmont today?"

"Do I look like the kinda guy who's gonna carry a tout sheet to a wake?" Foghorn rasps. "That would be most sacreligeous an' I am insulted that you would even think of me in that regard." Bein' spoken to in such a way actually makes Fats feel pretty good because he realizes at least he does not have to worry about gettin' kissed by Foghorn.

Goldie's mouth is now set in one very hard line an' she is tappin' her foot on the floor in a very steady beat that lets us know she is a very impatient doll at this moment. "If you do not let me speak you will not hear what I have to say." Nobody argued this point with her because it made a lot of sense, so she continues to talk, which she woulda done no matter what, because that is Goldie's way. She starts off by tellin' us about her cheesecake interview in Miami Beach which upsets the Clown so much that we all get speckled with tomato sauce when he starts sputterin' with a mouth full of lasagna (nothin' stops the Clown from eatin'), "You coulda become a tainted woman."

We are not payin' such great attention to the Clown's ranting right now as we are all very preoccupied pullin' out our handkerchiefs an' wipin' big red spots off our faces an' our nice new, hardly worn red plaid vests.

"If I get my hands around that bum Foxie Molloy's neck I will squeeze the life outta him!"

"Second place is not too bad," Goldie smirks. "You have been beaten to the punch, or maybe I should say the squeeze?" Suddenly we are payin' attention.

"Goldie, you are another Ma Barker!" Joey is shocked. "They will send ya to the electric chair!"

"If you do not keep quiet and let me tell what happened," she warns, "I really will wind up going to the electric chair. When Foxie sees I am a good girl from Hoboken who refuses to bring shame upon herself he calls out his so-called insurance agent and you will never believe who it was." Somewhere from the side of the room I hear what I swear sounds like, "Five'll getcha ten it is Louie the Louse."

I am not the only one who thinks he hears this but when our eyes turn in Fivel's direction he shrugs his shoulders an' says, "I didn't say anything." So we look back to Goldie for the answer because we have no idea who it can be. We know it cannot be whose name it sounded like we heard because we are at his wake right now.

It goes without saying, although it will be said, that we are greatly enlightened by what Goldie relates to us. In fact, she gets such a spell-bound audience, including Big Nose Sallie, you'd think we was at the finish line of a neck-and-neck stakes race instead of hearin' Goldie say that Foxie Molloy's insurance agent or enforcer really was Louie the Louse. This immediately curtails the consumption of food, even by the Clown an' Fats Suozzo, such activity bein' replaced by a most disorganized Question an' Answer session which is quickly shushed by a now very much in charge Goldie the Moderator, as well as chief speaker. She describes how it can be a very unsettling experience to come face-to-face with someone whose wake you have just been invited to attend. But, it seems, she is not the most unsettled person in the Sweet Stuff because when she explains to Louie the Louse that he is dead an' his wake is bein' held very shortly he is greatly saddened an' cannot believe that such a fate has befallen him. "Are you sure it is me an' not another

Louie the Louse who has come to such an untimely end?" It is more of
a plea than a question.

"What can be more definite than having a wake?" Goldie assures
him. "Have you ever heard of a wake for a live person?" While Goldie
is convincing Louie of his demise she begins wondering and questioning it herself and thinks of ways to check it out. Meanwhile, if no one
else is feelin' sorry for Louie there is still plenty of sympathy for his
situation even if all the tears bein' shed for him are his own. "I cannot
believe it," he moans, then feeling a sharp pain, grunts, "Ouch! It is so
very sad to think ... I will never have a gang of my own ... there will be
no little mahoscas to carry on my tradition ... What did I ever do to de-
serve such a fate?" At which point Goldie interrupts with, "Shall I start
with Roman numeral One, sub-paragraph A?"

"You should show more respect for the dead," Louie utters. "It is
such a shock to the system – it can kill ya." Another sharp pain, "Ouch!
I always thought ya felt no pain once you are dead."

"You probably would feel no pain," Foxie Molloy, who is enjoyin' this immensely, butts in," if Goldie stops stickin' you with a pin."
Goldie quickly pulls back the pin which she has very discretely been
jabbing into Louie as a test to see if he is truly dead.

"Owoo!" Louie cries, rubbin' his wounded thigh which had been
Goldie's target. "Will ya please quit stickin' me with that pin! Whatsa
matter with ya?" Goldie cannot believe it. Louie the Louse has failed
the bein' dead test. She cannot believe it because the Dwarf does not
make such mistakes. Maybe Louie is what is known as a zombie but
whatever Louie the Louse is, Goldie knows it is much healthier not to
be around him.

Louie squints very hard like he is tryin' to read very small print then
he looks up at the ceiling and finally at Goldie an' asks, "How come I am
down here in Miami an' they are havin' a wake for me in Coney Island?
Ain't I supposed to be laid out in a box at the front of the room or somethin'? How do they know I am dead if they cannot see my remains?"

"The same way they knew Knuckles McTavish and Honest Otto
were dead," Goldie zings it home. "Nobody ever saw them either."

"That is irrelevant. It is ancient history," Louie shoots back. "I am discussin' current events."

"Alright, I will fill you in. When Fivel zaps you," she explains, "he does such a job on you that nothing is left."

For a dead person, Louie's hair stands up very straight. "Who does what?"

"Fivel. Fivel Finnegan!" Goldie repeats. "I guess when you are dead your memory is not the same as when you are alive. Fivel is the one who knocked you off and the Dwarf agrees to pay him ten thousand dollars for this job. Naturally, the Dwarf being the shrewd article he is, says he must have your vest placed in his hands as proof ... " At this moment Goldie realizes something has gone wrong somewhere because Louie the Louse looks as bad as ever in his red plaid vest, which he should not be in at all because it is in the hands of Fivel Finnegan, soon to be handed over to the Dwarf.

Meanwhile, Louie is acting like a tea-kettle that has been whistling for ten minutes. "I do not mind bein' dead, but nobody's gonna make Ten G's over my dead body, especially that slimey weasel Fivel Finnegan - that money belongs to me – dead or alive!" He then turns to Foxie Molloy an' barks, "I need fare to get back to New York so I would like to be paid my first week in advance." Foxie laughs what turns out to be his last laugh an' says, "What does a ghost need money for? Anyhow we both know you ain't gonna be back." Foxie is still laughin' when he gets up and walks back to his office. Louie follows him back there an' as Goldie is high-tailin' it out of the Sweet Stuff she catches a glimpse of Louie the Louse comin' outta the office by himself countin' a fistful of greenbacks and she is quite certain that Knuckles and Otto have company.

When Goldie finishes tellin' us about how she spent her week in Miami Beach, Fats, who has great instinct for figurin' out how certain situations will develop, is very busily dashin' around the room scoopin' up all the food that he can stuff into his mouth an' what there is no room for in his mouth he is jammin' into his pockets until Vito collars him an' threatens to sew his mouth shut. Vito then turns toward Fivel who looks like he just spent a month in a bottle of Clorox, that is how white he is, an' hisses, "Who is gonna pay for this, Mr. Finnegan, as it don't look too good for you collectin' your Ten G's?"

"You are listenin' to an unsubstantiated report," Fivel snivels. "An' even if things do not work out right now for some unforeseen reason, I would give you my marker which is good anywhere."

"Fivel," Vito asks very calmly, "have you ever washed dishes?" Fivel is not exactly thrilled at the prospect of bein' a long-term dishwasher but he has much more serious considerations on his mind at this moment. While everyone else is busily discussin' the possibility of the Dwarf holdin' another lottery right now and wonderin' why he has not shown up yet, Fivel just wants to know where Louie the Louse is so he moves away from the wall that has been holdin' him up all this time an' tip-toes over to where Goldie an' Joey the Clown are engaged in what seems to be some very serious conversation. "What do you mean you did not re-member you had a wife?" Goldie's eyes have sparks shootin' from them an' both her hands are balled up into two little fists an' for a minute or so it looks like the Clown's head may become a punching bag. "You have known me for five years and in all that time you forgot you had a wife?"

Joey is in full retreat right now as he shrugs his shoulders an' stam-mers, "Well, sometimes I guess I remembered but it just never came up in conversation." Fivel is tryin' desperately to interrupt but he is bein' treated like a mosquito.

"Joseph DiCollona!" Hearin' Goldie call him that he knows he is in very big trouble. "I am a very well-brought up girl from Hoboken an' I have no intention of being known as a homewrecker!"

"There ain't no home to wreck," Joey whimpers, still in full retreat. Fivel is industriously tappin' both of them on their shoulders, but is still totally ignored except now he is bein' treated like a woodpecker.

"If you were a fisherman you'd probably be telling people how you caught a whale," Goldie declares with an angry toss of her head. "'No home to wreck'. As long as you have a wife you have a home to wreck."

"But I do not have a wife no more," the Clown replies, somewhere between a plea an' an explanation. "She has been converted to Security Deposit."

"' She has been converted to Security Deposit'?" More an' more Goldie is soundin' like a parrot. "This I gotta hear."

"Me, too," echoes Fivel, who for the moment almost forgets his own very major problem.

It is like the Clown senses this is make or break for him an' Goldie an' he turns in a performance that would not have been topped by John Barrymore or Laurence Olivier.

"For some reason I overlooked payin' our landlord rent the last three years an' him bein' a most heartless an' cruel human being, he strikes while the iron is hot. I shoulda known somethin' was up when our kitchen sink hadda be fixed four or five times a week. He spent a lot more time in our apartment than I ever did. Anyhow he works out a deal with my ol' lady, Angie, that he keeps her for the back rent and she keeps the apartment an' I am history. An' I am sure that the kitchen sink don't have to be fixed no more."

It is such a strong performance turned in by the Clown that both Goldie an' Fivel are red-eyed an' have tears streamin' down their cheeks. Goldie puts her arms around the Clown's neck an' very softly coos, "I guess you have awakened my maternal instinct, Joey. It is obvious you need someone to take care of you."

Joey's face creases into a smile, "Oh yeah. It is obvious. It is very obvious, Goldie."

"Excuse me for interruptin' such an emotional reunion," Fivel finally gets through, "but you never said what happens after you leave the 'Sweet Stuff'?"

"I pack my bags and catch the first train back to New York."

"An' do you have any idea what Louie's plans were?" Fivel asks, almost holdin' his breath.

"You are very fortunate, Fivel," Goldie states, "as you now have the opportunity to redeem yourself because Louie the Louse was very clear about his intentions to kill you. I am sure he wasted no time returning to New York. If he took a plane he could've gotten here before me."

Fivel becomes glassy-eyed an' rubber-kneed. "Oh, I am very fortunate. Thank you, Goldie. I am very, very fortunate." Fivel makes a bee-line for the telephone an' immediately calls the shop where the Widder Brown takes her calls. When they call Minnie to the phone, Fivel croaks, "It is a matter of life an' death that you get here immediately. Just put your foot down on the gas an' give it all you got."

"You're gonna have to wait, Fivel," Minnie explains. "I just got a call from the Dwarf who I have to pick up at the police station an' bring over to the Club for the wake."

"Oh, no, Minnie," Fivel is pleadin'. "Please get me first. Tell ya what. Pick me up an' I go with ya to pick up the Dwarf at the police station." Fivel cannot think of a safer place in the world for him to be right now than at the police station. He is even considerin' spittin' on the floor once they get there so maybe they'll keep him there for a few days.

Minnie hesitates for a moment. "I don't know, Fivel. I promised him I would be right over an' Mr. Langella is always very good to me."

"Minnie! Minnie!" Fivel is almost cryin' now. "Just go very fast an' we will be there in no time. I am tellin' ya, it is life an' death."

"That is usually the situation at a wake," she comments. "Okay, I am comin' to pick you up. I cannot stand to hear a grown man cry." Fivel knows that Louie the Louse would not come to get him at the Club because he could not risk the chance of the Dwarf bein' there but what Fivel does not know is that Louie the Louse makes a call to the police that morning and it is that call that causes the police to bring in the Dwarf. Since the stoolie does not show up an' the blood they find in the Dwarf's building turns out to be from a lamb they apologize to the Dwarf an' release him.

It is obvious that this wake is called off, hopefully just postponed temporarily, so we sit down an' start a friendly game of poker. Fivel Finnegan does not join in, over which fact no one is exactly broken-hearted. He is sittin' at the counter with his eyes on the front door, his knees knockin' like castanets. Goldie is helpin' Vito clean up the buffet tables, much to Fats' consternation, when suddenly Foghorn Manganaro bellows, "Wow! I do not believe it!" Everyone turns an' looks out the window of the Mermaid Social-Athletic Club. There, racin' down the middle of Mermaid Avenue, is a guy dressed like all the rest of us – in a red plaid vest. Only he is like an enraged bull except no enraged bull I ever saw was able to wave a cannon over its head. It is very obvious that Louie the Louse has become a maniac on a mission. Nobody knows too good exactly what happens next because we are all trippin' over each other scramblin' to get outta the way. Fivel doesn't know at all because he goes into a dead faint.

What all of us remember is there is this long, loud screech of rubber on pavement and this is followed by the horrendous crunching and smashing of metal an' glass. Nobody moves or says anything for a very long moment because we are all waiting for the imminent arrival of our unwanted guest, Louie the Louse, but he does not put in an appearance – yet. It is Minnie Brown who finally opens the front door an' walks in, breakin' our open-mouthed silence. "Are any of you boys mechanical, maybe. My cab seems to be broken down."

We all very gingerly step outta the Club, not knowin' what to expect. The Clown is the first one to correctly analyze the situation. "I do not think you will be able to drive the car as your radiator an' grille are bashed in an' your headlights are broken." Hooked over the hood ornament was a red plaid vest, not in very good condition an' off to the side of the cab was what was left of Louie the Louse. Just then another cab pulls up an' out steps the Dwarf. Big Nose Sallie immediately rushes to his side an' would've whispered in his ear except he couldn't reach it so he talks very softly to the Dwarf, obviously apprising him of the day's happenings.

"Oh, Donato," Minnie apologizes, "I was on my way to pick you up when my cab broke."

"That is okay, Minnie," the Dwarf assures her. "Goldie, why don't you take Minnie inside an' give her a hot cup of coffee while we move her cab." As he says this he plucks the vest from the hood of the cab.

"I guess we gotta report this, huh, Boss?" Fats asks.

The Dwarf looks around. "Report what. These pot-holes are all over the place. What are we gonna report?"

Everyone shakes his head in agreement that these pot-holes are terrible.

"But what about Louie the Louse?" Fats asks, pointing at the lump by the curb.

"What about him?" the Dwarf answers. "Everyone knows we had his wake today. It's about time the guest of honor shows up. Carry him inside and call Laurenzo's Funeral Parlor. Tell them we need one oversized casket and they will have to do their work on the premises."

"I knew it," Vito shakes his fist in disgust. "I just finish packin' all the food away an' cleanin' up; now I gotta set up all over again. Do me a favor. Next time get Junior's to cater your wakes – not just the cheesecake.

The second wake for Louie the Louse is a very joyous occasion, much moreso than the first. Also, the Dwarf feels much better about the way everything develops. He never did feel too good about orderin' the rubout of Louie. He knew that for the good of everyone it was necessary but he does not feel too comfortable bein' responsible for someone's demise, even a lowlife such as Louie the Louse, may he rest in peace, but not too well. As it turns out, Louie winds up the victim of an accident so the Dwarf's hands and conscience are completely clean.

You shoulda seen the Widder Brown when the Boss tells her she is the winner of our Club's ten thousand dollar treasure hunt because of the red plaid vest that winds up on the hood ornament of her cab. "Everybody has a red plaid vest. How come this one is the winner?" she asks in amazement.

Big Nose Sallie answers, "Because this is the one, the only an' the original that belonged to the late Louie the Louse."

Minnie beams, "If only my Herman were here to see this. This is one wake he woulda enjoyed more than his own. How did Louie check out, anyhow?" she asks as an afterthought.

The Dwarf looks at her an' answers, "He was a notorious jay-walker, Minnie. It finally caught up with him." Once again I see what I suspect is a smile on the Dwarf's face. The Dwarf tells Minnie that with so much money now she can go get an operation to remove her cataracts an' be able to see again.

Minnie thinks for a minute, then she reaches up an' actually gives the Dwarf a pinch on the cheek. "Ya know, Donato, you are really a very good man, only you don't like no one to know it. I am very happy with the world that I see, but I may not be as happy if I see too much. I think I will leave my world the way it is. Maybe I won't drive my cab anymore. Now that I am an executive I will get someone else to drive it while I concentrate on my newspaper business. Maybe I will even upgrade an' start sellin' today's paper, who knows. It'll be good to have some free time to take a walk now an' then."

The Dwarf sounds different than I have ever heard him before. "I like to take a walk once in a while myself, Minnie. Would ya mind if we take a walk together sometimes?"

"Only if you promise to walk very slow, Donato. You know, you take much bigger steps than I do."

I gotta say, things are much more relaxed around here now. The Clown musta gone to obedience school because even though Goldie does not get a leash for him he is always at her side an' heels an' sits an' maybe even rolls over when he is supposed to. If he had a tail it would definetly be waggin' at full speed.

Nobody sees anything of Fivel since the night of Louie's demise. When we get back into the Club he is already gone. Word has it that he is livin' year-round with his sister Flossie in Miami which is okay with me as nobody ever accuses me of not enjoyin' a good poker game anymore.

———————————————

www.ingramcontent.com/pod-product-compliance
Lightning Source LLC
Chambersburg PA
CBHW071228260626
47162CB00004B/1463